"You know I lo
Marry me, Stella."

She wished Russ hadn't stopped touching her. Gavin had said, "He'll keep you dangling until he's put a wedding ring on your finger." Even now he was leaving her longing for more while he waited for her answer.

Shamelessly she pressed herself against him, her lips touching the beating pulse at the base of his throat. "Not marriage, Russ," she whispered.

"You won't marry me," Russ said harshly. "But you're willing to sleep with me."

Stella nodded. His crude words made her offer sound cheap and sordid.

Then Russ pressed her head back unbearably. It was a kiss without tenderness, and when he moved his hand over her, his touch was rough and insulting.

"Thanks for the free sample." He released her—and left without another word.

Books by Daphne Clair

These books may be available at your local bookseller.

For a list of all titles currently available,
send your name and address to:

Harlequin Reader Service
P.O. Box 52040, Phoenix, AZ 85072-2040
Canadian address: P.O. Box 2800, Postal Station A,
5170 Yonge St., Willowdale, Ont. M2N 5T5

DAPHNE CLAIR

take hold of tomorrow

Harlequin Books

TORONTO • NEW YORK • LONDON
AMSTERDAM • PARIS • SYDNEY • HAMBURG
STOCKHOLM • ATHENS • TOKYO • MILAN

Harlequin Presents first edition August 1984
ISBN 0-373-10711-0

Original hardcover edition published in 1984
by Mills & Boon Limited

CHAPTER ONE

THE day was going to be one of those still and shimmery ones when the harbour reflected fragments of light from the sun, and the graceful cone of Ragintoto floated on the green waters of the Waitemata Harbour like a mythical island from a James Michener vision of the South Seas. But in High Street the tall office buildings blocked the sun, except for fitful patches stealing around corners, and the crowds of office workers and early shoppers, legal staff and students—for the courts and the University of Auckland were both nearby—didn't seem to notice the narrow strip of clear blue sky, their eyes on the even narrower grey pavement under their hurrying feet.

Pausing for an instant on the threshold of one of the offices, the young woman in the smart dark blue linen suit worn with a crisp white blouse and navy shoes looked down the slope of the street and took a deep breath, then smiled at herself, the firm line of her mouth curving, and her cool blue eyes softening. She might fancy that, along with the fumes from the traffic already roaring up and down Queen Street only metres away, she could detect a whiff of sea air, but she knew perfectly well that from here the harbour which met the bottom of Auckland's main shopping centre was invisible.

Sighing, and yet feeling an inexplicable lifting of a heart that had been a leaden weight in her chest for two years, Stella pushed through the swing doors and crossed the red-tiled lobby section of the Rawson Building, smiled a greeting to Michelle at Reception in answer to her, 'Good morning, Mrs

Rawson,' and ran lightly up the carpeted stairs to the first floor.

Her personal secretary looked up from opening the mail as Stella entered the outer office, and said, 'Mr Armstrong is waiting to see you, Mrs Rawson.'

'Thanks, June. Bring the mail through when you're ready.'

Owen Armstrong was leaning against the window frame behind her desk, admiring the view of the multi-storey car-park he could see through a gap in the buildings, or perhaps the glimpses of the Waitemata that could just be discerned between its concrete floors. His tall, thin frame was loosely encased in a brown suit with a blue shirt, and his tie, as usual, was both unsuitable and askew.

Stella blinked at the green-on-yellow pattern of what appeared to be a species of slightly deformed pine tree, and hastily averted her eyes to the Company Secretary's long, intelligent face. 'Good morning, Owen. You're early.'

He straightened and ambled over to her, just too late to help her take off her jacket, and stood by as she hung it with her tooled leather shoulder bag on the elegant cane rack in one corner.

'You're late,' he argued amiably.

Stella glanced at the large 'man's' gold watch on her wrist, and said firmly, 'Nine o'clock.'

'Two minutes past,' Owen told her smugly, referring to the electronic clock on the wall opposite her desk.

Stella laughed and settled herself in her chair. 'All right, you win,' she conceded, ostentatiously altering the time on her watch. 'Sit down.'

'When's the new boy coming?' Owen asked, taking one of the green velvet-upholstered chairs facing the desk.

'I told him to see me at nine-fifteen,' she said,

picking up a file folder that June had placed ready for her. 'Want to read this again?'

Owen leaned over, glanced at the name on the cover and sat back. 'No, thanks. I can remember the salient points well enough, and whizz-kids make me feel my years.'

'Do you think that's what he is?'

'He got the job of Project Manager over ten others, didn't he? And some of them, I seem to recall, had pretty good track records. If it hadn't been for your determined lobbying, the board would have chosen one of the others. In fact . . .' Owen coughed and shifted in his chair. 'Anyway——'

But Stella stopped him, her eyes suddenly sharp. 'In fact, what?'

'Nothing, just something Jepson said.'

'What did he say?' Her eyebrows rose in amused curiosity.

'You don't want to hear it.'

'Oh, do stop pussyfooting, Owen! You might as well tell me now.'

'Well, some of the board members are a bit surprised at your pushing so hard for Russ Langford to have the job. They reckon experience counts.'

'Russ Langford *has* experience. He's had a very thorough grounding in all aspects of computer technology, training in America, working for a software development firm, in charge of technical services at his last job——'

'Yes, I know. But he's only twenty-five, Stella.'

'Well, he's packed a lot into the last few years.'

'Why did you push for him?' Owen asked bluntly.

Stella regarded him shrewdly, the light from the window behind her highlighting the few strands of blonde hair that had escaped the smooth styling of her chignon, her eyes clear as blue glass. 'What does Gavin think?' she asked him. 'That I fell for a pretty face?'

Owen coughed again. 'He didn't put it in those words, exactly——'

'I see.' Icily she continued, 'I wanted Russ Langford for Project Manager because I feel he's the best qualified for the job. He's young enough to bring a fresh approach to a new field, and experienced enough to know what he's doing. He also had the courtesy to look me in the eye at the board interview and address his answer to my questions to me, not to the nearest male face. I won't take on employees who look on me as either a decorative figurehead for the company, or a sort of freak whom they don't know whether to address as "Sir" or "Madam", which is how most of the applicants seemed to see me. I found his attitude refreshing, but even that wouldn't have cut any ice if I hadn't thought he was the best man for the job. Being female doesn't make me incapable of adopting an objective viewpoint.'

'You don't have to convince me, Stella,' Owen protested. 'I'm on your side.'

'Sorry, I didn't mean to take it out on you.'

'Pity Gavin Jepson isn't here in person.'

'Oh, that man!' Stella burst out, and her hands, resting on the immaculate blotter before her, balled into fists. 'To think that Mark was actually friendly with him! I wish he wasn't on the Board, but Mark wanted him——'

'He's a very knowledgeable bloke.'

'About business, maybe. He knows nothing about women! He's a male chauvinist of the worst kind——'

'It's his business ability that Mark wanted. I don't suppose Jepson's views of women in business really mattered.'

Stella sighed. 'No, he couldn't have foreseen that he would die at only forty-two and leave me to carry on, with Jepson doing his damnedest to show me up as ineffectual, simply because I happen to be female.

Does he really think I'd be stupid enough to take on someone as vital as Project Manager because I liked the colour of his *eyes*?' She paused. 'I can't even remember what colour they were, can you?'

Owen grinned and shook his head. 'I'm not a woman. On the other hand, I would say that he was more than averagely endowed as far as looks go.'

'I did happen to notice that Mr Langford was better looking than most of them,' Stella admitted. 'Jepson, too, obviously didn't miss *that*, but surely even he doesn't think I'm a cradle-snatcher? I'm twenty-nine, for heaven's sake! And he knows perfectly well I've not looked at any other man since Mark died.'

'Maybe it's time you did.'

'What?' Stella's head jerked up, her eyes chilly with hauteur.

Owen smiled wryly. 'Just a thought. Twenty-nine isn't exactly one foot in the grave, you know, Stella.' He paused. 'Gavin Jepson, for one, wouldn't mind you sending a glance or two in his direction.

Her lip curled with scorn. 'He'd be the last—the very last man I'd look at—if I was looking at all.'

'Where does that leave *me*, then? Second to last?'

'Oh, don't be silly!' Stella said irritably. She picked up the file on Russ Langford, and Owen sat regarding his shoes, his long legs stretched out before him. Something about his pose arrested her gaze, and she stared at him with a faint sense of shock. She thought of Owen as one of her very best friends. After Mark's dreadfully sudden death from a heart attack, Owen had been a tower of strength and earned her undying gratitude and affection. He had guided her in the early months of taking over the reins of the company Mark had built, and been a buffer between her and the more sceptical board members until she felt strong enough and competent enough to fight her own battles. He had supported her first efforts to assert her right to be more than a token figure on the board, and had argued strongly for her when she expressed her intention of taking her late husband's place as the Managing Director of the company he had founded.

It had never occurred to her before that Owen's devotion held more than loyalty to the memory of the man who had given him the chance to use his amazing ability to organise company affairs, and a mild fondness for herself. Now, when he looked up at her, she found herself recognising something deeper in his brown eyes.

'Owen?' she said uncertainly.

He smiled wryly. 'How about dinner tonight?' he said with kind of stubborn embarrassment.

'Yes, of course,' she said quickly, then looked up with relief as June tapped on the door and came in to deposit the opened mail on her desk. 'Excuse me a minute, Owen,' Stella murmured, glad to be able to transfer her attention to the pile of letters. She handed June one or two to deal with and dismissed her with a smile.

Owen cleared his throat and tugged ineffectually at the dreadful tie, bringing it to an ever more rakish angle against the front of his blue shirt. Another time she would have said, 'Here, let me,' and adjusted it for him with casual affection. But today an element of constraint prevailed. Tonight wouldn't be the first time they had dined together, but somehow in the last few minutes a subtle shift had taken place in their relationship. She was not yet sure how to deal with it.

June again tapped on the door, and opened it to say, 'Mr Langford's here, Mrs Rawson.'

'Thank you, June. Come in, Mr Langford,' she added as June stepped out of the way to allow the tall, dark-haired young man to enter the room. His eyes, she noticed irrelevantly, were blue, but quite unlike her own. They were a deeper colour, almost grey, and they met hers directly under straight black brows. He wore a neat charcoal-coloured three-piece suit that she now remembered from his interview, with a dark red tie, and he looked businesslike and alert.

'You remember Owen Armstrong?' she murmured, as the two men shook hands. 'Please sit down.'

He took the chair next to Owen's, sitting in a relaxed way, but not lounging, and she said, 'I've asked Owen to fill you in on the financial side of the project you'll be engaged on first, and then I'll take you round the departments myself and introduce you to other members of the staff.'

The deep blue eyes showed a flicker of surprise, but he said quietly, 'Thank you, Mrs Rawson. That's nice of you.'

'I do it for all our new employees,' she said, a faint hint of sharpness in her voice.

His eyes held hers a moment longer, then switched to Owen as the Company Secretary embarked on a succinct rundown of the funds available for different sections of the project for which Russ Langford was to be responsible. It involved the supplying of tailor-made computer systems to farmers by means of which they could keep track of the complex information needed about stock rotation, feeding, breeding pro-grammes and a variety of operations necessary for economical and productive agriculture. One of the things which had made Russ Langford's application attractive enough for the board to shortlist his name had been some months he had spent on a Canadian farm helping to operate their computerised system of stock and pasture control.

While Owen went on with his explanations, Stella had time to watch the new man unobserved. He was, she had to admit, almost too good-looking, his hair not quite curling, but looking as though it would need only the slightest encouragement to do so, and the

square chin just saving him from having a face like a
Greek god. She thought at first that he looked older
than twenty-five, but then decided it was his air of
quiet and almost casual assurance that gave that
impression. From his face she would have found it
difficult to guess at his age—would probably have
said, vaguely, in his twenties, and left it at that.

At that moment he glanced up at her, an eyebrow
just barely lifting in enquiry, his mouth curving in a
half smile, and she just stopped herself from returning
the smile. Having Gavin Jepson making snide remarks
about her choosing the new man for his handsome face
was bad enough. If Langford himself thought her
susceptible, the situation would become impossible.
With his looks young Langford was probably
accustomed to females of all ages falling at his feet.
She would be wise to disabuse him very rapidly of any
idea that she might be ready to do the same.

So when she took him about the various departments, introducing him to the heads of accounting,
sales, service, and project development, she was brisk
and businesslike, giving him time to chat for a short
while to the other staff members as they went, but
setting a fast pace in the corridors between the
sections.

When they arrived at the office set aside for him, he
said, 'Thank you very much, Mrs Rawson. Do you
always move at that speed?'

His smile was disarming, his head held slightly to
one side, inviting her to smile back. He had charm, she
thought dispassionately, and was probably used to
getting results with it.

Returning his look coolly, she said, 'I like to get
things done, Mr Langford, and don't believe in
wasting time. You'll learn that we do things smartly
here. Now, would you like to meet your own staff?'

For a moment he didn't answer, his direct look

unexpectedly disconcerting. 'I won't take up any more of your time,' he answered smoothly. 'I guess I can introduce myself. Thank you again, Mrs Rawson.'

It was a dismissal, she realised, taken aback. Perfectly polite and respectful, but a definite dismissal, none the less. He was taking charge of his own office and his staff, and letting her—the boss—know that she wasn't needed any longer.

Her brows rose, and involuntarily she felt the corners of her mouth and eyes turn up with humour. 'I think you'll cope very well,' she said somewhat dryly, 'but please don't hesitate to come to me or any of the heads of department if you have a query or a problem.'

He nodded. 'I appreciate that.' Then he stood by his new desk waiting for her to go.

Back in her own office, Stella reflected that in spite of his relative youth, the new Project Manager looked like being quite able to take charge of the job with a maximum of speed and efficiency. She certainly hoped so, because she didn't want Gavin Jepson having any reason to repeat his offensive hints about her supposed personal interest.

Gavin Jepson himself called in later in the morning, entering her office after a cursory tap on the door, having walked past June without enquiry, a practice which always annoyed her, and taking his welcome for granted. As usual he bypassed the two chairs for visitors, to lean on the corner of her desk instead, his leg suggestively close to hers as he folded his arms and looked down at her with a gleam in his dark eyes, and waited for her to acknowledge him.

Quite apart from his manners, which Stella thought left much to be desired, he was a difficult man to ignore. Tall and deep-chested, with the broad shoulders of a rugby forward, and the sort of tough good looks that got television actors starring roles as detective heroes, he exuded a deliberate and cultivated aura of masculine power and confidence. His tan, although he spent most of his time at various board meetings or in his own downtown office, was deep and apparently permanent, probably, Stella decided, acquired by hours spent under a sun-lamp. Where the other directors appeared at board meetings in business suits and ties, or, in the height of summer, walk shorts and neat open-necked shirts with folded-back collars, Gavin affected fitting body shirts undone almost to the waist, and metal medallions, of which he appeared to have a wide selection. He also, Stella had decided sourly, thought himself God's gift to womankind, although he regarded women themselves as pretty, brainless toys. No wonder his marriage, which had apparently broken up some time in the dim and distant past, had not lasted!

Stella, entering the firm as a computer demonstrator fresh from business college, had become her husband's personal assistant when they married, and afterwards Mark had made her a director. It was in this capacity that she had first clashed with Gavin Jepson, who had obviously thought the appointment merely a formality, and had simply ignored any opinion she put forward, until Mark made it clear that she was a full working director of the company. Stella gathered that he had then decided Mark was simply besotted, and he treated them both thereafter with mild contempt, which irritated Stella immensely, though Mark had been merely amused.

'Poor old Gavin,' Mark had said. 'I'm afraid his broken marriage has soured him on women.'

'Nonsense,' Stella had retorted. 'His impossible attitude to women probably broke up his marriage in the first place. No woman could live with a man like that!'

She had not changed her opinion, although since her husband's death she had come to reluctantly concede that Mark had been right about Gavin's business acumen. He had other business interests of his own, and was a valued member of the board. She had to admit that the others listened to him when he talked finance and development. He was brilliant in his field, and she tried to respect that, and ignore the fact that she found him personally abrasive.

'How's the new boy settling in?' he asked her now, the gleam in his eyes intensifying as he waited for her answer. The usual medallion was nestling in a tangle of chest hair, level with her eyes. It seemed to be Indian, and depicted in graphic detail what was probably a copy of a temple carving. The temple, she guessed, had been dedicated to some Indian god of love. Stella averted her eyes.

'Fine,' she said. 'And he's hardly a boy.'

Gavin grinned. 'He's too young for you, darling.'

'Don't be stupid!' Stella snapped.

She saw the angry tightening of his mouth before he said softly, 'Getting sensitive about your age, Stella? You needn't worry, you're still a beautiful woman. But don't waste it on youngsters like Russ Langford. If you're ready to start looking around again, there are bigger fish in the sea.'

She stared at him, nearly speechless with furious disbelief. He looked back at her with a half smile, his eyes deliberately going over her, giving her the full battery of what he obviously thought of as his overpowering sexual magnetism.

'Like you?' she asked him derisively. 'No, thanks. And I'm *not* looking round.'

'Aren't you?' His sceptical look was a masterpiece. 'It's been two years, and I'd take a bet you're not frigid, darling, in spite of your iceberg looks. They say the cold ones have fire underneath, and I'll bet Mark found it, didn't he? He wasn't a man who would settle for less than a woman was capable of giving him.'

'That is none of your business! How dare you sit here in my office and——' Her face flushed with temper, Stella put her hands on the desk in front of her and made to rise, but before she could do so, he had leaned down, catching her chin in his hand, and was kissing her.

Stella was so astonished that for a second she didn't move. Then, as her hands came up from the desk to his shoulders to push him away, she dimly heard the door opening, and a moment later she was free.

She saw June's surprised face, and behind her Russ Langford. She realised that although Gavin had got off the desk, and was standing behind her chair to face the door, his hands were on her shoulders, the fingers moving caressingly.

As he removed them, he answered June's flustered, 'I'm sorry,' easily, saying, 'That okay, I'm leaving now. 'Bye, darling . . .'

That last was for her, Stella realised, a deliberate red rag of masculine teasing . . . or else he was trying to stake a claim. No matter which, it infuriated her further. She felt like throwing something after him.

Instead she said with as much composure as she could muster, 'That's all right, June. You wanted to see me, Mr Langford?'

She met his eyes briefly, expecting to see them full of curiosity, and was held instead by the total blankness of his expression, his eyes shuttered. He said, 'I thought you might want to see the time plan I've drawn up for the project.'

'Already?' Her surprise showed as she motioned him to a chair.

'I made a tentative one over the last two weeks while I waited to take up the appointment,' he said, 'and now I've talked it over with the staff you've given me, there are some alterations. So it may look a bit rough at the moment, but I'd like to give you the general picture . . .'

'By all means,' she said. 'Let's see it.'

She spent the next half hour with him, impressed by his grasp of detail and the quick assessment he had made of the thrust of the project.

'I need to do some field research,' he said at the end of the session, folding up the plan. 'I know you have made some preliminary contact with interested parties, farmers' groups, etcetera, but I'd like to see at first hand some of the farms that may eventually make use of the system, and talk to the farmers themselves about their ideas of what's needed.

'Yes, of course. There's a company car at your disposal at any time. It goes with the job, of course, as you know. Fix it up with Owen Armstrong.'

'Right. Thank you, Mrs Rawson.'

When he had gone, June came in, saying, 'I'm awfully sorry about that, Stella. I didn't know Mr Jepson was here—he must have come in just as I'd slipped out to the ladies'.'

'That's all right, June. It wasn't your fault. And for the record, I didn't ask that man to kiss me, nor did I enjoy it. And I know I don't need to tell you not to mention it to anyone.'

'Of course I won't. Er—what about Mr Langford?'

Stella looked rueful. 'I had to pretend he hadn't seen anything. I couldn't very well start explaining to him——'

'No, it's a bit awkward isn't it? Still, I don't suppose he'll go spreading it around, do you?'

'No.' He was a bright young man with better things to do, she hoped, and he'd hardly been in the office five minutes, scarcely long enough to know anyone to spread gossip to even if he was so inclined. Anyway, she consoled herself, if he thought she had accepted

Gavin's kiss willingly, it might help to disabuse him of any idea that she had hired him because he had attracted her himself.

June was still standing before the desk, looking at her curiously.

'Something else?' Stella asked.

'No—at least——'

'Yes?'

A little mischievously, June said, 'Are you sure you didn't enjoy it? Mr Jepson's quite a hunk of man.'

'June!' Stella said threateningly, and the secretary laughed. She had worked for Mark before Stella took over, and the two women had always got on well, although in the office they usually preserved a formality that went by the board at other times.

'Well,' said June now, 'sorry if I'm speaking out of turn, but you're young to stay a widow. I know you've not looked at anyone since you married Mark, but believe me, dear, there's plenty that are looking at you. Maybe Gavin Jepson decided to wake you up to the fact.'

'I take it you think it wasn't a bad idea?' Stella said wrathfully.

'Well, it's time somebody did. Running a company is all very well, but it's not much of a life without someone to care for.'

'I don't think I can care for anyone the way I did for Mark,' Stella said quietly. 'And I wouldn't want to short-change a man who loved me.'

'Well,' June admitted, 'Mark was quite a guy. And maybe the man wouldn't mind.'

'Maybe,' Stella said noncommittally. 'Now, can we get on with the letters? I have some replies to make to these component manufacturers who tendered for the mini-computer disk drives.'

CHAPTER TWO

THE dinner with Owen was less than successful. Stella was unsettled by the events of the day and her sudden realisation that Owen felt deeper than liking, and Gavin Jepson anything other than tolerant male contempt, for her. Owen had never before hinted at more than liking and sympathy, and while Gavin had an automatic reaction to any reasonably good-looking woman, a repertoire of gleamingly suggestive glances, slyly sexual remarks and apparently accidental touches, he had never made a direct attack on her. She wondered if something in herself had made them both bold enough to reveal their thoughts, or if she had been lacking in perception.

She much preferred Owen's diffident approach to Gavin's male aggression, but tonight Owen was trying too hard. The restaurant was not one of the quiet places with good food they had been to before, but a very high-class establishment with acres of white starched tablecloths and waiters to match, and a menacing regiment of silverware at each side of their plates, seemingly designed for a ten-course dinner.

The menu presented for her inspection lacked a list of prices, but the names of some dishes indicated their probable cost, and when she heard Owen order the wine she blinked, knowing perfectly well that the price for that particular French vintage was something over twenty dollars for a bottle.

'I'm rather fond of some local wines, myself,' she said tentatively.

'Yes, I know Mark was a connoisseur of New Zealand wines,' Owen said rather grandly, 'but tonight

I want something extra special. I'd like this evening to be memorable.'

Her heart sinking slightly, Stella smiled and was silent. She hoped that Owen hadn't been building up fantasies about her and their relationship. She valued his friendship, but as for anything else between them, she couldn't imagine it. He was a sweet and clever man, but she didn't see herself straightening his impossible ties and listening to his economic theories for the rest of her life. And she knew him too well to imagine he had anything less than permanence in mind. It was a pity his wife had died and left him childless. Stella had never met her, but Owen had once shown her a photograph, and Mrs Armstrong had looked pretty and goodhumoured and capable, a perfect foil for him.

After pressing far too much food on her, and happily discussing politics, economics and company affairs all evening, he took her home, pressed a quick, clumsy kiss on her mouth, and left her at her door torn between vexed laughter and a sort of guilty exasperation. She didn't know at all what she was going to do about him.

She joined the new Project Manager for lunch in the staff dining room on his second day. It was her custom to do so with new staff members in a conscious effort to make them feel welcome and also find out something about their personal background. Mark had not been good at these personal touches, and with the firm rapidly expanding from small beginnings at the time of their marriage, had been toying with the notion of employing a personnel manager. Instead, he had noted Stella's ability to get on with people and take an interest in their welfare, and given her, as his personal assistant, a special responsibility for liaising between him and the staff. After his death she had preferred to preserve her own personal contact with them, and had found it a definite asset that she was able to maintain friendly relationships at every level. Still smarting from Gavin Jepson's insinuations, she had for the first time been tempted to drop the practice of lunching with the latest addition to the staff, but in the end decided that to be influenced in that way would play into Gavin's hands.

However, she found the lunch unexpectedly difficult. In her manner there was a constraint that she could not shake off. She found herself mentally vetting each question to ensure it could not convey a too personal interest, and she felt that Russ Langford was humouring her. He answered her questions politely enough, but seemed as if he didn't want to give too much of himself away. He had no brothers but two married sisters, one older and one younger, and his mother worked in a solicitor's office. His father had died three years ago when he was in America. It was one of the reasons he had come home.

Somehow getting the feeling he resented giving the information, Stella said, with a smile that she realised was stiff. 'This is a friendly company, and we like to know a little about our staff. We want them to feel at home.'

He nodded an acknowledgement, but didn't give an opinion on that. Nor did he smile. Slightly exasperated, she added formally, 'I hope you're going to enjoy working with us—most of our people stay quite a long time.'

He nodded again, then looked at her in the oddly direct way she had noticed before, as though he was trying to see behind her eyes. 'I intend to see the project through,' he said.

'Well,' said Stella, unreasonably irritated, 'I'm glad. I'm sure you won't be sorry you came here.'

He smiled then, and again she was conscious of the

definite male attraction he possessed, not blatantly cultivated like Gavin's macho image, but more subtle and insidious. 'Thank you, Mrs Rawson,' he said, and for the first time she saw in his eyes a warmth that acknowledged her sex.

Made sensitive to such nuances by the events of the day before, she froze. Surely he hadn't read more into her innocent remark than she had meant? 'Of course,' she said crisply, 'we—the company—will expect a lot from you. You're very young for the position we've given you, and I hope that you're able to live up to our confidence in you—as a Manager.'

He looked slightly amused, then, but his faint smile faded as he said, 'I shouldn't worry, Mrs Rawson. Your confidence isn't misplaced.'

'You're very assured for your age,' she commented dryly.

'Twenty-five isn't so young in the world of computers, Mrs Rawson, as I'm sure you know. It's a young man's—or woman's—game.'

'Yes,' she agreed, aware that in America, particularly, college graduates were sought after and paid high salaries for working in the very competitive computer technology development industry. 'But I wouldn't call it a game, exactly. We have a lot of money invested in this project——'

'And you want results,' he finished for her. 'Don't worry, Mrs Rawson, you'll get them. When I promise, I deliver.'

He sounded ultra-confident, but not as though he was boasting. He had, she knew, a quite formidable brain. Perhaps that was what gave him an assurance beyond his years.

As though he read her mind, he said, 'I wish you'd forget about my age. You can't be much older yourself, anyway.'

'I'm nearly thirty.'

He didn't say, 'You don't look it,' but merely nodded as though she had confirmed a guess.

Somewhat tartly, she added, 'Women are more mature than men at the same age, anyway,' and then wondered why on earth she had volunteered that bit of popular psychology.

'So they say,' he agreed, 'but I've never gone along with that theory, myself.'

'Really?' She gave him a cool smile and pushed her chair back. 'I must get back to my office.'

Standing politely, he said, 'That's a shame. The conversation was just getting interesting.' There was laughter in his eyes, and she looked back at him frigidly. His brows rose faintly, and the laughter died. As she swept past him, he bowed his head very slightly with a distinct air of mockery.

Russ Langford quickly found his feet in the company, and Stella was able to breathe a sigh of relief that her judgment had not been at fault. His immediate staff, she noticed had accepted his authority without a murmur, although many of them were older than their boss. As well as a thorough grounding in electronics, he seemed to have the ability to deal with people and get the best from them. And he seldom asked anyone for help or advice. Apparently he didn't need it.

She herself had kept deliberately aloof from him for the most part since that lunch. She had no intention of giving Gavin further grounds for suspicion of her motives, and neither did she want Russ Langford to think she had any personal interest in him.

Each year the anniversary of the founding of the company was celebrated with a staff party. It was a tradition begun by Mark Rawson, and although the first year after his death the occasion had inevitably been marked by sadness, Stella had been determined that it would go ahead.

This year's party, she had decided, was to be bigger and better than ever. The staff dining-room was transformed into a cabaret-style setting, a dance band was engaged, and the caterers instructed to provide a lavish buffet.

Stella had bought no new clothes since being widowed, excepting a few businesslike blouses and skirts, but now she decided to shop for something fresh and pretty to grace the staff party. Looking round the boutiques in Parnell, where the old buildings had been refurbished and restored in Colonial style, she found a chiffon dress in sandy gold, with cord straps over the shoulders, a satin underslip and a narrow skirt softened by a tiered layer over it. Worn with bronze sandals and a topaz pendant necklet and earrings set which had been a birthday present from Mark, it looked glamorous and suitable, and she entered the dining room on Owen Armstrong's arm with the pleasant anticipation of a woman who knows she looks good.

She had hardly had time for one glass of wine before Gavin Jepson claimed her for a dance. He held her tightly, his eyes devouring her so openly that she couldn't help a faint heat rising in her cheeks, which he eyed with some satisfaction. 'You've been keeping me at arms' length long enough, Stella,' he said, his mouth just brushing her temple. 'Why go on with the act?'

'I'm not acting,' she said coldly.

'You're blushing. At your age, that has to mean something more than mere shyness.'

'I'm simply embarrassed at being made conspicuous. You're holding me far too closely.'

'I'd like to hold you closer still, you know that.' His hands moved insinuatingly, and Stella stopped dancing and said between her teeth, 'Let go, Gavin. I've had enough!'

He laughed softly. 'Sure?'

Twisting out of his arms, she turned to go back to the table where the directors and their wives sat.

Another pair of arms came round her as she collided with a hard masculine chest.

'Sorry, Mrs Rawson,' said Russ Langford, his hands surprisingly strong as he stood her away from him.

'It's all right,' she muttered, more scarlet-cheeked now than ever. 'My fault.'

She was aware of his eyes going from her to Gavin, and had the feeling that he was filing information away like one of their own computers, making rapid calculations and coming up with some predictable answers. She wished he wouldn't always seem to be around when Gavin Jepson had put her in an embarrassing situation. It was beginning to become a habit.

'Perhaps you'd dance with me later, Mrs Rawson?' Russ Langford said suddenly, surprising her.

She felt Gavin's hand possessively on her waist, and some instinct for self-preservation made her say warmly, 'Yes, of course, Russ. I think it's time we dispensed with the formality, you know. Senior staff usually call me Stella.'

There was something about the short silence he allowed to lapse then that brought an unexpected twinge of unease. 'Thank you,' he murmured, then flickered a swift glance at Gavin, and stepped aside for them to move past him.

Stella sat between Owen and Gavin, feeling like a bone between two dogs. Not that Owen had the slightest inclination towards snarling; nor did Gavin, she was sure, have any idea that Owen could be a rival. His arrogance wouldn't have recognised Owen's brand of devotion as a threat. He didn't even take her own resistance seriously. When he pressed his thigh against hers under the table and she pointedly shifted her leg away, he merely grinned, and threw his arm across the back of her chair. Her turned shoulder didn't stop him brushing his thumb over her bare upper arm. In desperation she was driven to asking one of the other directors to dance with her, leaving his dumpy little wife glowering at them from the table, apparently under the impression that Stella had taken a fancy to her husband.

Since the director was rather portly himself, and bald as well, Stella wondered at the jealousy she was obviously arousing in his wife's ample bosom, but perhaps the man had hidden charms. She herself had known him for five years and found him almost totally charmless. But then maybe she lacked taste. She had to admit that Gavin Jepson had everything a woman was supposed to want in a man, and yet she disliked him intensely, and even dear Owen, with his gentleness, patience and undoubted intelligence, failed to stir her emotions to anything more than a lukewarm fondness.

Mark had been the only man ever to do so, and Mark was gone . . .

Sharply she stopped herself from travelling down that road. Memories were precious, and there were times when remembering was good for the soul, bringing comfort and solacing loneliness, but this was not one of them. Tonight was a celebration of all that Mark had worked for and that she had carried on in his name, a time for fun and laughter and a sense of comradeship among people who worked together every day, and who were now being invited to relax and play together in the interests of the company. It was to reward them for loyalty and hard work, and to encourage them to continue their efforts in the future.

But she found that tonight the memory of her husband became intrusive, and everywhere she looked she saw the evidence of his presence. Even the prints that hung on the walls had been chosen by Mark. He had been interested in art, and had had an insatiable desire to put his own individual stamp on everything he did, so that although a firm of very good decorators were called in to furnish the offices when they were built, they had worked closely with him and followed his ideas rather than being given carte blanche.

He had been an admirer of Rei Hamon's work even before it became universally known, and some of the Maori artist's distinctive black-and-white prints of bush scenes hung behind the canteen counter, which was transformed into a bar for the night. Looking at them, even while she admired the finely drawn ferns and creepers and the intricate curve of a curled ponga frond, Stella began to feel sadness creeping over her, and in an effort to lighten her mood allowed Gavin to fill her glass again and again with champagne, drinking rather more than she normally would have.

When Russ Langford came to claim his dance, she smiled at him brilliantly as she rose and took the hand he held out to her, and once more experienced that strange constraint, as he looked back at her almost watchfully before leading her to the floor and taking her confidently in his arms.

Many of the other couples were dancing either apart or with arms wound round each other, but he held her correctly just inches from his body, one hand on her waist and the other holding hers. He was a good dancer, though, and after they had settled into the rhythm and adjusted their steps to each other, he began to add fancy touches, his hand firm as he guided her into more complicated manoeuvres.

'Where did you learn to dance?' she asked him, rather amused. 'I thought boys these days didn't bother with ballroom steps.'

He glanced down at her and said, 'My mother did

competition ballroom dancing for years. She taught me. Not that I'm up to competition standard, of course.'

'But you enjoy it?' she guessed shrewdly. No one as good as he was could deny that.

'Yes,' he said briefly. 'My mother had a theory that a sense of rhythm and a head for mathematics go together.' He swooped into a smooth reverse turn and glide, so that she had to concentrate to follow him, which she did faultlessly.

'Ever done disco dancing?' he asked her, as he settled into a more conventional quickstep.

'Yes. Mark loved it—my husband. Perhaps your mother was right in her theory.'

The music had changed to a fast disco beat, and he said, 'Are you game—Stella?'

Before she could reply, he had swung her away from him with one hand, and was smiling a challenge at her even as her feet automatically began responding to his lead and to the beat of the music.

A few other couples tried to follow suit, but soon Stella was aware that they had the floor to themselves, the band playing for them alone. He was really extremely good, his improvisations graceful and not too showy, and he didn't go off into his own private dance, but kept her whirling to him and back again, definitely a twosome, but with himself very much in control of their movements. It was exhilarating and great fun, and she finished, finally, breathless and laughing as Russ held her across his arm, the band playing a drum flourish and the admiring crowd about them applauding loudly.

Looking down at her flushed face, he said, 'Thank you. Can I get you a drink?'

'I must look as though I need one,' she said ruefully, putting a hand to her hair. 'I think I'm too old for this sort of thing.'

'Don't be ridiculous,' he said rather shortly. 'And stop fiddling with your hair. It's fine.'

He took her arm and they went to the bar, where he got her a lemonade and something golden and sparkling for himself.

Rather coldly, she said, 'I was drinking champagne, actually.'

'I noticed,' he said. 'Do you want another one?'

'No,' she admitted reluctantly. 'What's that?' pointing to his glass.

'Ginger ale. I want a clear head, too.'

'Who said I did?' she enquired.

He looked at her steadily, and then a faint smile touched his mouth. 'Do you want to go back to the stuffed shirts?' he asked her.

Sipping on her lemonade, she nearly choked, trying not to laugh out loud. 'They're not stuffed shirts.'

He grinned down at her. 'Come and sit at our table for a while,' he suggested. 'After all, this do is supposed to allow you to hobnob with the lower orders, isn't it? I bet you'd have a lot more fun.'

'Mr Langford, I don't——'

'I thought it was going to be Russ tonight. Or was that only for Gavin Jepson's benefit?'

'I've no idea what you mean——'

'Yes you do, but let it pass. Are you coming?'

'All right,' Stella said weakly, suddenly unable to bear the thought of the rest of the evening fending off Gavin and trying to avoid Owen's soulfully hurt gaze. 'For a little while.'

The people sitting at his table were mostly technicians and programmers from his department, but she recognised some of the girls as the demonstration and tuition specialists who operated the computers and showed new users how they worked.

They were on average much younger than the people at the directors' table, and she found herself stimulated by their conversation and their enthusiasm. She knew all of them by name, and there was no stiffness in their welcome, they seemed glad to have her with them. A whole hour passed before she had realised it, and she was having a laughing argument with one of the technicians about a recent film and their different interpretations of it when Owen, his long face unusually disapproving, interrupted her.

'Time for your annual speech, Stella,' he reminded her. 'You want to get it in before people start to go home, don't you?'

It was another tradition begun by Mark, of course. The short résumé of what the company had achieved in the past year, and a brief exhortation to continue its undoubted success into the next, followed by a toast to the future.

Reluctantly, Stella rose and accompanied Owen back to the microphone in front of the band. She had prepared the short talk well and spoke without notes, but although the crowd gave her a reverent silence, and she didn't stumble over her words, they came out to her own ears as meaningless and hollow. She looked around the big room, her gaze lighting on one face after another, trying to infuse some sincerity into what she was saying, and finally came to rest on Russ Langford. He was lounging back in his chair, rocking it slightly on its back legs, his arms folded, and she thought at first he looked bored. Then he smiled at her, and looked straight into her eyes, and suddenly her words took on life and meaning as she spoke to him.

Departing from the set speech near the end, she said simply how proud she was of her late husband's achievement, and how she wanted to live up to what he had started, not only in terms of material success, but in meeting the challenge of the unknown future, being part of a new industrial revolution which would see uses for computer technology hardly yet dreamed of, in science, in medicine, in education and in vast unexplored fields of human endeavour, as well as in commerce and, their newest venture, agriculture. She touched on the fears of some sectors of the work force that they would be ousted from their jobs by computers, and expressed the hope and conviction that, on the contrary, more and better jobs could result from computers taking over the duller, repetitive tasks while people were freed for more creative and interesting work. With proper attention paid to phasing in new technologies and re-training workers, she suggested, the advent of progress could be smooth and beneficial to all. Change was an inevitable part of growth, and human society was a living entity that without change and growth was doomed to stagnation and death.

Finally she proposed the toast to the future and sat down to more than polite applause, and Owen, who had guided her inexorably back to her proper place, patted her shoulder, saying gruffly, 'Good speech, Stella. Mark would be proud of you.'

Gavin raised his glass to her and said, 'Yes, that should rouse the troops to greater endeavours and more profits, Stella. Congratulations.'

The evening, after that, was soon over, and she let Owen drive her home, in spite of Gavin's offer to do so.

'A lady goes home with the man who brought her,' she said lightly, brushing him off.

'A lady would have stayed by her escort, wouldn't she?' he retorted. 'You went off with your new Project Manager for nearly an hour.'

'The whole idea of this party is to allow *all* the staff to mingle and get together on a social basis.'

'I didn't see you doing much mingling while you were sitting with your pretty boy,' he retorted.

'He is not a pretty boy!' Stella flashed, furious. 'And I was sitting with a group, as you very well know.'

'He wouldn't satisfy you, darling. You're a woman, and you need a man, not a callow youth.'

Stella's skin crawled. She was tempted to hit him and be hanged to the gossip it would create. Fortunately Owen joined them then and, seemingly happily ignorant of any tension, said goodnight to Gavin and took her out to his car.

CHAPTER THREE

An old friend of Mark's who was into farming on a large scale had contacted Stella, asking about computerisation. It looked like an ideal opening for the new project, and she sent for Russ to tell him about it.

'Warwick McLeod owns a complex of dairy and mixed farms in the Waikato,' she explained, after letting him read the letter she had received. 'Tarahanga Farms. Have you heard of them?'

'Can't say I have.' He handed the letter back. 'It sounds like a big outfit.'

'It is. I think that if he's willing to work in with us, this could be a golden opportunity to actually try out the new hardware and software as we go, and it could benefit both Warwick and us, in the long run. He's going to be in Auckland next week and will be coming in to see me. I suggest you sit in on the meeting. If I make a time will you keep it free?'

'Of course. Does he know anything about computers?'

'I don't know. Probably not much, I think. But he's a very up-to-date person, he may have been doing some reading on the subject. I wouldn't assume he's an ignoramus.'

'I won't.' He sounded rather dry, and she looked at him sharply, only to find him regarding her with the bland expression she always found so disconcerting because it hid his thoughts completely.

Warwick was not ignorant. He admitted that his knowledge was basic and gleaned mainly from magazine articles, but when Russ asked him if he understood how computers worked, the big, tanned farmer grinned and said, 'Well, as I see it, a computer is a machine that deals in a code made up of various combinations of 1 and 0.'

'The binary code,' said Russ nodding.

'And the key to the modern micro-computers is the silicon chip that we hear so much about,' Warwick continued. 'It's a simple little slice of silicon that can be engraved with complicated electronic circuits in miniature, so that it can store and process coded information. How am I doing so far?'

'Top of the class,' Russ grinned.

'So the way the computer works is basically dumb. It only knows two things, 1 and 0. But it can do things with them so fast, combining them in different ways and converting the coded numbers into symbols like numbers and letters, that it seems intelligent.'

'I guess that's one way of putting it, Mr McLeod. And you're right—a computer's arithmetic is really very simple-minded, it's the speed that makes it seem smarter than us.'

'As far as I can make it out, the tricky bit is communicating with the thing to tell it what you want it to do. The computer deals in code, isn't that so?'

'Yes, but as you obviously know, there are ways of programming a computer to translate commands into its own binary language and carry them out,' Russ explained.

'Ah, this is one of the things I'm not too sure about,' said Warwick, leaning forward. 'There seem to be a number of computer languages—why not just one? Surely that would make sense?'

'Well, some have been developed for specific purposes, Mr McLeod. Others are meant to be improvements on what has been used before. Basic is the most widely used general-purpose one, which I'm sure you've heard of.'

Warwick nodded.

'Fortran is a computer language developed for scientists' needs; it's largely based on algebra. And Cobol was designed with the business world in mind—its full name is Common Business Oriented Language.'

'What about a farmers' language, then?' Warwick asked. 'Has anyone come up with that yet?'

'Not to my knowledge, though a number of programs for farmers written in other machine languages are being used overseas, and some specifically for New Zealand use are in the process of development here.'

Stella broke in. 'The thing is, Warwick, you don't need to know a computer language at all, as a user of a properly designed system. You might save some money if you learned to programme a computer yourself in one of the computer languages, but it would take a great deal of time. We're just beginning a project to develop farm-orientated systems, and we hope to provide farmers with computer hardware and software tailored to their needs, with ready-made programs which they can use easily without learning any coded language.'

'Hardware and software?'

'Sorry,' Stella smiled. 'We get used to the jargon here. Hardware is, loosely speaking, the machinery, the boxes, that house the computer parts. You would have a keyboard, a VDU screen—that's a Video Display Unit, very like a TV receiver—and a disk drive unit, which houses the disks used to record and read programs that can be fed into the computer. The basis of the system is a central processing unit which processes information keyed in by the user and then "outputs" it in readable form. The disk drive will

accept disks programmed to allow it to carry out
certain functions, and also record on other disks
information which you ask the computer to store in its
electronic filing system. Software refers to things like
the disks themselves, that store programs and that can
be altered and modified by programmers to specific
uses. It can also refer to tapes which some machines
use for a storage medium, and can even be used on
printed programs which can be keyed in to a computer
in one of the coded languages.'

'I'm told it's important to have a computer with a
large memory capacity,' Warwick commented.

'It can be,' Stella answered. There are two kinds of
memory, the permanent instructions "burned in"
during the manufacturing process, which cannot be
changed—that's called ROM for Read Only Memory,
and it can be programmed for specific applications like
word processing, or set up in one of the special
computer languages, so that it "understands" Basic or
Cobol, or whatever, without the need for re-
programming each time it's switched on.'

'And the other kind of memory?'

'RAM, or Random Access Memory. This is what
makes computers so versatile. It's a volatile memory
which can be erased and re-programmed for specific
applications. It's software accessible.'

'So,' said Warwick, 'the same machine could be
used by a businessman or a farmer, using different
programmes stored in the software?'

'Yes,' said Stella. 'But we hope to choose the best
hardware for the job, perhaps modify it if necessary by
altering it and adding new chips, and develop a software
program to complement it.'

Warwick looked sceptical. 'I don't know that
computer programmers know enough about farming
to come up with what someone like me would need.'

Russ leaned forward. 'That's where your input on

this program could be very useful, if you're willing.'

Stella said, 'We're hoping, Warwick, that you'll work with us on this project to some extent, let us develop a system especially for you, based on your assessment of what you need.'

'Well,' Warwick sat back, running his fingers reflectively over his chin, 'that makes sense. Only how long will it take to give me a system that's up and running?'

Russ said, 'I'd hope, less than six months. In fact, in much less time than that, you could be running the first programs, and we'll undertake to modify them as we go along, according to your specifications. You could go to one of a couple of firms that have farm programs for sale now, spend between six and ten thousand dollars, and have a system plugged in within a few weeks, but the program would be an adaptation of one designed for America, Europe or possibly Australia. We think we can do better than that, and for less money.'

Warwick looked thoughtful for a few moments, then said, 'That sounds fair enough.'

'Of course you'd get a substantial discount, in view of the fact that you'd be helping us to develop the program,' Stella assured him.

'I'm sure I'll get a fair deal from you, Stella,' he said. 'Mark was always reliable in business, and I know you are too.'

'Thank you. Could Russ come down to Tarahanga some time soon and consult with you? An on-the-spot report seems a good idea.'

'Yes, it does. I'd like you to come too, Stella. Marianne hasn't seen you for ages. Why don't you both come, perhaps Friday, and stay for a weekend? That's if you don't mind combining business with a social visit. Say next week?'

Stella hesitated. It meant travelling with Russ Langford, giving fuel to any gossip there might be . . .

But there were no grounds for gossip, and if Warwick had invited her alone she would have accepted. Why should she give up something she would have enjoyed, just because of Gavin Jepson's silly suspicions?

'Thank you,' she said, 'I'd love to come. Will that suit you, Russ?'

'Fine. I'll look forward to it, Mr McLeod.'

'Warwick.' The farmer stood up and held out his hand. 'I'll see you, then, Friday week. Stella knows where to find us.'

Stella decided to use her own car for the trip. She took the wheel, and Russ sat beside her. It was a glorious summer day, and as she gained the southern motorway out of the city her heart lifted at the prospect of three days in the Waikato, the golden heart of the North Island. She and Mark had spent several very pleasant weekends at Tarahanga after their marriage.

'Marianne's a marvellous cook,' she said to Russ. 'You'll enjoy your meals.'

'She's Warwick's wife, I take it?'

'That's right.'

'Any children?'

'Four. Two of them are away now, one in Australia and one at university.'

'Girls or boys?' he asked.

'The two eldest are girls, the ones still at home are boys, Wayne and Kevin. Wayne will be a teenager now, and Kevin would be—about ten, I think. It's a rather spread out family.'

'Do you have children, Stella?' asked Russ.

'No,' she answered shortly.

She would have liked children; they had talked about it, but had kept putting it off. Mark had so much to do, had said he wanted to build up the business to the point where he could relax a little and enjoy a family when they had one . . .

They passed the suburban outskirts, the bunches of new houses with their backs to the motorway, nappies flapping on rotary clothes lines, and newly planted trees that barely reached the windowsills. Then they were in rolling hill country, the cattle and sheep grazing grass that was beginning to green again after a few days of heavy showers following weeks of dry summer weather.

The motorway proper ended just before they reached the Bombay hills, where a strong Indian community had established market gardens on the rich volcanic soil, and fruit and vegetable stalls ranging from humble trucks parked by the roadside to large supermarket type greengroceries were found every few hundred yards.

The road climbed to the summit and gave them a lovely view of the valley ahead, backdropped by graceful blue-hazed mountains, before sweeping them downhill.

'I've always loved that view,' Stella murmured, almost to herself, as she changed gear and slowed the car to admire it.

'This is a beautiful country,' said Russ.

'You're not hankering to return to the States?' she asked, casting him a curious glance.

He shook his head. 'Not really. It's exciting, stimulating, and I liked the people, but——' he shrugged, 'I guess there's no place like home.'

'Tell me about America,' she said. 'I've never been there.'

She didn't see the look he threw at her before he obeyed. Then he began to talk, and she listened with increasing interest, encouraging him with frequent questions. They passed through several small towns without her really noticing, so that she was surprised to find that they had reached Huntly, the old coalmining centre, in what seemed a very short time. At Ngaruawahia, as they passed over the bridge into the town, he asked, 'Would you like me to take a turn at the wheel?'

'I like driving,' she said, 'but you can if you like.'

She drew up at the side of the road and he got out and came round to the driver's side while she slid across the seat.

'It's almost lunch time,' he said, as he opened the driver's door.

'I thought we'd wait until we got to Hamilton.'

'Okay.' He got in and started the car smoothly.

'But if you're very hungry——' Stella said. 'After all, I suppose you're a growing boy.'

It was a feeble joke, but she had expected him to at least smile. She gathered from his silence and the tightening of his jaw muscles that he was annoyed. On other occasions when she had mentioned his age, he had reacted with a mixture of amusement and exasperation. It seemed the exasperation this time was uppermost. She must remember not to tease.

He drove fast and competently, only slowing when they reached the outskirts of the city. 'Stay this side of the river?' he asked her.

'Yes. We'll find somewhere to eat in the main street, if you can park.'

'How about a picnic?' he suggested, adding dryly, 'children like them, you know.'

'It sounds a good idea,' she answered. 'It's much too hot to eat inside.'

'Okay.' He found a parking space and stopped the engine. 'Stay there,' he said, touching her wrist as she made to move. 'I'll get it.'

He was gone before she could protest, and she shrugged mentally, wound the window down and waited.

It was a good fifteen minutes before he returned with two large paper bags and deposited them on the back seat.

'The river or the lake?' he asked, his hand on the ignition.

'Oh—the lake, I think.' At least she was getting a choice there, although he hadn't asked her what she would like for her lunch.

But there was a delicious aroma coming from the bags in the back, making her mouth water.

They found a spot under trees near the lake, and Russ took a clear plastic pack from one of the bags and opened it to spread a plastic tablecloth out with a flourish on the grass.

Stella looked at it with incredulous amusement. 'You bought a *tablecloth*?'

'Like it?' he grinned, eyeing the rather violent design of enormous yellow daisies.

'Well,' she said doubtfully, 'in this context it's—er—colourful.'

He laughed, his dark eyes glowing with humour. He motioned her to sit on the grass, and went to get their lunch from the car.

When he had it arrayed before them, she looked at it with awe. He had bought paper plates and plastic forks, and even some clear plastic wine 'glasses' which he laid out before displaying the food—and drink. Sparkling white wine for the glasses, a whole cooked chicken, ready-made salads in plastic containers, crisp fresh bread rolls, tiny pats of butter in foil and a slab of cheesecake.

'Your kind of picnic?' he asked her.

'Definitely my kind of picnic,' she answered firmly, her lips curving. Then, as she lifted the wine he had poured for her, she looked at him more searchingly and wondered if he had thought she would turn her nose up at sandwiches and soft drinks.

Russ ate more than she did, but she found her appetite larger than she would have expected. The meal seemed delicious, and she enjoyed every mouthful.

'You'd better put in a meal requisition slip for this,' she reminded him. 'I suppose you didn't get receipts?'

He looked up from pouring the last of the wine, his eyes oddly sharp. 'No.'

'Well, I'll see you get recompensed,' she promised.

He leaned back against the tree, regarding her with slightly pursed lips. 'Okay,' he said, 'if you insist.'

He sounded decidedly cool, and Stella explained 'This is a business trip, after all. You're entitled to claim for any expenses.'

'Okay, boss,' he drawled, making her look at him quickly.

'I don't care for that form of address,' she said. 'I told you to call me Stella.'

'Yes—Stella.' He made it sound like 'boss.'

Restlessly, she looked about, and he said, jerking his head, 'It's over there.'

She instinctively looked where he had indicated and saw the brown wooden building further along the lake shore.

'Thank you.' She got up and, taking her handbag, walked away from him.

The facilities were clean, if simple. She combed her hair and renewed her lipstick, then strolled along the lake edge to rejoin Russ. He had packed up the picnic, but was lying on the grass, his head pillowed on his hands, watching her approach.

Something about the way he watched made her selfconscious, and she stood by him, saying abruptly, 'We'd better be getting on.'

He got up without comment and, opening the passenger door, waited for her to get in. He hadn't asked if she wanted him to drive the rest of the way but then, she reminded herself, they had changed over not so long ago.

She slid into the seat and did up her safety belt. When Russ started the car she asked, 'Do you know how to get there?'

'I looked at the map. If I'm not sure I'll ask you.'

He didn't need to ask until they were almost there, when she directed him down a side road lined with poplars. The road wound gently uphill, and eventually brought them to a wooden gate set in a post and rail fence, and bearing a plaque with 'Tarahanga Farms' printed on it. A pepper tree dipped its branches over one gatepost, and a rural delivery mailbox, painted bright red and with 'McLeod' neatly lettered on its side, was firmly fixed to the other.

The main house was enclosed by a white picket fence with trees and shrubs pressing against its palings. The building itself was long and low, white too, with blue windowsills and a dark blue roof.

Russ stopped the car on a rise just before they reached the drive to the house. 'So that's where the name "Tarahanga" came from.' He leaned across her to point at the long low saddle between two hills that rose behind the farm house. 'Tarahanga—the saddle of the hill.'

Stella turned her head to follow his gaze. His hand fell, grazing her thigh as he shifted back into his seat. She felt her cheeks burn, and kept her face averted from him, hoping he hadn't noticed.

'Oh, yes,' she said. 'Warwick told me that the first time I came here with Mark. I scarcely know any Maori,' she added. 'Where did you learn it?'

'At school. I was one of only three Pakeha kids at a very small rural school. I couldn't help picking up some Maori, when practically everyone in the community spoke it.'

Interested, she dared to look round at him. 'And you still remember it?'

'The odd word or phrase comes back to me. It's a shame it's not spoken more—our indigenous language.'

'Yes. I've often thought I'd like to learn it.'

'There's still time.'

'Perhaps.' He hadn't meant to touch her, she knew, but for some reason she was very conscious of his closeness, his hand resting on the seat behind her, his thigh a hairsbreadth from hers. Crisply she said, 'Hadn't we better be moving on?'

He started the engine again without a word, and took them down the hill to the farm.

Marianne came out to meet them, her plump figure a testament to her own cooking, her pretty face wearing a smile of genuine welcome.

She embraced Stella and shook hands with Russ and ushered them into the house, Russ carrying his and Stella's overnight bags.

'We've put you in the girls' room, Stella,' she said. 'And Russ can have the guest room. Would you mind showing Russ—I've got some scones in the oven and that's the bell going now to take them out.'

'Fresh scones,' Russ murmured as he followed Stella down the wide hall. 'I can hardly wait!'

'We've barely had lunch,' she protested, as she opened the door of the room Debbie and Susan had shared before they left home. 'I'll take that bag now.'

But he walked in and deposited it at the foot of one of the beds, looking at its flowered, frilly spread. 'As you said, I'm a growing boy,' he told her.

'I thought I'd offended you, at the time.'

'So what's new?' he shrugged. 'Where's the guest room?'

'Across the hall. What do you mean?'

'Thanks. I'll find my way.'

He made to pass her, and she said sharply, 'Just a minute!'

'Yes?' He was quite close to her, and she realised with a shock how tall he was—not excessively so, but enough that she had to look up to him when he stood this near.

'You sounded as though you often take offence at what I say.'

'Now, that would be over-sensitive of me, wouldn't it?' he asked gently.

Nonplussed, Stella didn't know what to say, and after a moment he swung on his heel and left her, closing the door behind him.

When she went into the kitchen to find Marianne, she discovered him there before her, hoeing into a fresh scone dripping with butter, while Marianne turned an enormous roast of mutton at the oven.

'Have a scone, Stella,' Marianne invited her, and Russ, his mouth full, pushed the plate over to her, along with a dish of butter.

She hadn't been hungry, but the sight of the lovely golden-brown rounds was too much. She buttered one and bit into it, closing her eyes in ecstasy at the warm, featherlight deliciousness of it.

When she opened them, Russ was grinning at her across the table. 'And who's just had lunch, then?' he teased.

Her eyes smiled back at him as she wiped a small drip of butter from her chin. 'I told you about Marianne's cooking,' she said, after swallowing the next mouthful. 'It's irresistible.'

'I'll second that.' He reached for another scone as Marianne said, 'There's a pot of tea going for anyone that wants it. And I see Warwick just coming across the paddock now.'

When, after a leisurely afternoon tea, Warwick offered to take them both for a walk round the farm,

Stella looked at Marianne and asked, 'Do you need help with cooking the dinner?'

'No, dear. I know you love the farm. Go with the men and enjoy yourself.'

'Well, let me set the table when we get back, anyway,' said Stella, and added to Warwick, 'I'll just change my shoes.'

In the bedroom she kicked off the high-heeled pumps and pulled a pair of espadrilles from her case. In winter she would have had to borrow a pair of rubber boots from the row out on the back porch, but in this weather the espadrilles should suffice. Her linen skirt and shortsleeved shirt were all right, she decided, but she rolled off her tights before donning the casual shoes.

Russ had been wearing a cream cotton knit shirt and fitting khaki drill slacks all day, and when she joined the men on the porch she saw that he had borrowed some boots. His gaze swept over her, and she saw the corners of his eyes crinkle, although his mouth remained firm and grave. Nettled, she looked down at herself, then up at him, her brows rising in enquiry. He shook his head slightly and stepped back to let her follow Warwick first down the steps.

The ground was firm, with new green shoots coming up through dry, stiff grass. Looking down as they walked through the paddocks, she could see tiny wild flowers nestled in the grass under their feet, little blooms of purple, blue, yellow and pink, and small red and green grasshoppers clinging to bending stalks. The cattle eyed them curiously as they passed, and the sheep stared and ran, their rumps bobbing comically. Stella knew she ought to be listening to the explanations Warwick was giving them about controlled grazing and stock ratios, because they needed all the information they could get, but her mind kept wandering, giving in to the sheer enjoyment of the hazy summer afternoon, the distant rasping song of cicadas in a patch of needle-leaved totaras further up the hill, the sight of a hawk hovering and wheeling over the saddlebacked hill, the fresh smell of a row of pine trees bordering one of the paddocks.

Warwick opened gates for her, but at one point he had built a sturdy stile in the middle of a particularly long stretch of fence.

Russ went over first, skipping the lower step on the other side to land lightly on the ground. Warwick put a hand under Stella's elbow as she went up the two steps. Holding her skirt with one hand, because the stile was narrow and crossed a strand of barbed wire that was part of the fence, she balanced herself at the top ready for Russ to hold out his hand and help her down. Instead, she felt strong fingers gripping her waist as he swung her down easily and set her on her feet.

Startled, she looked up and found him looking back at her with a strangely tense expression. The pupils of his eyes were extended in the deep blue irises, and the skin over his cheekbones looked suddenly taut. Her breath seemed to stick momentarily in her throat. Then he let her go, and Warwick thudded down beside them and they went on.

How stupid, she said to herself blankly, as she lagged slightly behind the two men, and watched Russ, his head turned slightly as he listened intently to what Warwick was saying. For a moment there she had felt a purely primitive feminine thrill at the strength of him as he held her. It was just, she thought, that no man had touched her like that since Mark . . .

Like what? It had been a casual gesture, merely helping a woman over a gate, and he had let her go immediately she was steady on her feet. She had surely imagined that strange expression on his face.

They stopped at the top of the rise, and leaned on a wooden railed gate in the fence which crossed it, to look back towards the house. Warwick pointed out different sections of the farm, and she tried to look intelligent and take it all in. Russ was asking questions that seemed to make sense.

Warwick said, 'I'll just take a look at that sheep over there. Don't like the way she's limping.'

'Can I help?' Russ asked him.

'No, it's okay. You two could find your way back to the house, if you like. I think I'll check the gully now that I've come this far.'

They watched him as he approached the sheep quietly, expertly moving her before him into a corner of the fenceline, and catching her just as she tried to limp away past him. He turned her gently, and after a minute or so let her go, then continued on his way.

Russ, leaning back against the gate, said, 'Shall we go?'

'Yes, I promised to set the table for Marianne. Did you take in everything he said?'

'Most of it, I think. Did you?'

Tempted to lie, Stella finally opted for the truth, and shook her head. 'A lot of the time I was wool-gathering. The country has that effect on me. Business seems unimportant when I can breathe fresh air and smell the grass and listen to the cicadas bursting with song.'

He grinned. 'I thought you looked a bit bemused and uninterested. 'You didn't even try to concentrate, did you?'

Suddenly lighthearted, she grinned back at him. 'That's what I pay you for!'

His eyes lit with laughter, he said, 'Yes, ma'am.'

'And,' she said tartly, as he opened the gate for her to let her walk through, 'you needn't come that meek act with me. I suspect you're just as much of a male chauvinist underneath as—as anyone.'

He looked at her with lifted brows but said nothing as he fastened the gate.

When he came beside her, she asked abruptly, 'What was so funny about me when I came out of the house?'

'Nothing.'

'Oh, come on, you could hardly keep from laughing. I want to know why.'

'Is that an order?' he asked smoothly.

Turning to face him, she looked up into a hard, steady gaze. Gazing back equally steadily, she said defiantly, 'Yes, if you like.'

'Okay. I thought I'd never seen a real live woman looking so much like a *Vogue* magazine idea of what the well-dressed lady wears in the country.'

Stiffly, she said, 'Well, I'm sorry if you don't approve——'

'I didn't say that. You look stunning. As always.'

Taken aback, she said, 'Well—well, thank you.'

'That's all right. Why are you looking so surprised? You must be used to compliments.'

She had had her far share, of course. But this one had taken her unawares. 'I suppose,' she said, trying to pass it off with laughter, 'that I don't expect to get them from—from younger men.'

'Younger men have eyes, too,' he said. 'How old was your husband?'

CHAPTER FOUR

STELLA stopped abruptly to stare at him, and with a wry look he said, 'Is that stepping out of line?'

'He was forty-two when he died,' she said, her voice chilly.

'That was only a couple of years ago, wasn't it?'

'Yes.'

'Then he was much older than you.'

'Fifteen years. I'm sure you've done the arithmetic.'

Russ inclined his head. 'I didn't mean to upset you.'

'I'm not upset. I just don't happen to think that my husband's age—or mine—is any of your business.'

'Okay.' His eyes gleamed. 'But you told me all the same.'

'I can't think why.'

'You couldn't help yourself,' he suggested solemnly. 'I have that effect on people.'

Stella tried to hold on to her anger and failed. Reluctantly, she laughed in answer to the humour in his eyes, and they walked on together.

The house came into view as they breasted a rise. A mixture of young oaks and flowering shrubs and trees overhung its surrounding fence, and the swimming pool in one corner of the section shimmered in the sun.

'I didn't realise they had a pool,' Russ commented, 'until we were looking down on it from up the hill, there.'

'The heart of the Waikato is a long way from the sea,' Stella reminded him. 'It isn't like the North, where a good beach is usually within easy driving distance. Did you brings togs?'

'Yes. Are you going to swim?'

'Probably.'

She did, after setting the table for Marianne and being told there was nothing more to do but wait for Warwick to come in, when the meal would be ready for dishing up. The two boys had arrived in the school bus and were doing chores and homework. They had, Marianne told her, had a quick swim first.

The pool was deliciously inviting after the hot afternoon, the ferns planted about the edge of it, at the foot of surrounding trees, adding to its charm. Russ was already in the water when she arrived in her white bikini and cotton towelling wrapover. He reached the other end of the pool in a leisurely crawl, and turned to face her as she slipped the jacket off.

She stepped on the tiled edge, and hesitated. Russ was silent, and she looked up to see him staring with unashamed interest, his gaze moving up her long legs to the small triangle of cloth, then past her waist to her breasts, and finally meeting her eyes.

'Come on,' he said quietly, his voice carrying clearly. 'Take the plunge.'

For a moment longer their eyes locked, and then Stella swung her arms up and dived cleanly, swimming underwater to emerge in the middle of the pool.

He had swum to meet her, and was waiting for her when she surfaced. Again his eyes seemed to challenge her, but she avoided the challenge, turning away from him to swim to the side, then going underwater again to the other side.

He didn't follow, but when she came up again he was sitting on the tiles at the end, watching her. She tried to ignore him, swimming slowly to the other end, then doing a fast crawl the length of the pool. As she turned to swim back, she felt the splash as Russ landed beside her, and in a second realised he was racing her.

She was a strong, fast swimmer, and a sudden shot of adrenalin seemed to give her an extra spurt. They reached the end together, their hands touching the tiles at the same moment, and she turned breathlessly to look at him, shaking the water from her eyes, seeing his white smile, his hair sleek with the water, his eyes laughing at her.

'You're good,' he said.

Recklessly, she answered, 'Teach you to respect your employer!' and smiled at him, teasing.

He grinned back. 'Yes, ma'am,' he said, tugging at his wet forelock in mock humility.

Stella lifted a hand and swiped it over the surface of the water, splashing him, but he retaliated with far more force, until she had to give in, cowering with her hands over her face and laughingly begging him to stop.

When he did, she turned on her back and floated lazily, gazing up at the sky, which was still blue and pulsating with heat. Daylight saving would carry on until March, and it wouldn't be dark until nearly nine tonight.

Warwick joined them for ten minutes, and then Marianne sent Kevin to call that dinner was almost ready, and they went in to dress.

Over dinner, Stella took more notice of the discussion than she had that afternoon. Russ was suggesting ways in which a computer system could be used to calculate the amount of feed likely to be available in the paddocks at different times, and how herd movements could be controlled, also on computer advice, to make the best possible use of the available grass.

Wayne, who as a sixth-former had been learning the use of computers at school, asked some intelligent questions about the proposed programs, and Russ, treating him as an equal, embarked on a discussion of programming methods which threatened to become rather technical.

Marianne broke in to ask if the computer would be able to do the farm accounts, a job which she undertook for Warwick, and Stella answered her, 'It won't do everything for you, you would still have to enter the amounts in the right places, just as you do in your account books now, but the computer can do the calculations very quickly and accurately once the figures are programmed into it, and give you a neat print-out afterwards. It would certainly make accounting easier. And it will be able to work out a farm budget based on the variables that you state in the program, and even work out a cash-flow forecast based on data from past seasons.'

'That would help if we wanted to borrow any capital for improvements, Warwick,' Marianne observed, turning to her husband.

'Will it play Space Invaders?' young Kevin wanted to know.

Russ grinned. 'You can buy games ready-made to feed into most computers, but you'll have to ask your father if you're allowed to use it for that.'

'We'll talk about that another time,' Warwick told his son. 'Wait until I find out more about what we really want to use it for, first. You were saying something about recording liveweight gains,' he reminded Russ. 'Now that interests me. If the computer keeps track of which animals are in peak condition and ready for sale . . .'

'No problem, I'm sure,' Russ answered. 'In some countries, they're already using computers for actually conducting stock sales, did you know that?'

Warwick shook his head. 'I don't see how.'

'Well, it takes a computer hook-up. The information on stock for sale is fed into a computer which is interfaced with another central computer that collects the information from the sellers, then lists it for the buyers, and at an agreed date and agreed location the stock is inspected by the buyers or agents, and the sale conducted by computer hookup. Some stock may even change hands several times before moving from the farm. It saves a lot of transport costs, and of course the loss of condition that often occurs with shifting livestock from place to place, and sometimes having to take the animals home again if there's no sale.'

'Well, it certainly is a different world,' said Marianne, beginning to stack their empty plates. 'Just ten years ago, the thought of having a computer sitting in Warwick's office would have been something out of science fiction. Now I can even believe that in another ten years we might be buying and selling stock by pushing keys. Anything seems possible.'

Stella said, 'The thing is to turn the changes to good account for your purposes, Marianne, not just stand still and let them leave you behind in yesterday's world. Still, stock-buying and selling by computer is in the more distant future. At the moment what we ought to be doing is identifying Warwick's immediate needs and seeing what we can do to start filling them.'

'Right,' Russ agreed. 'I suggest we have a good look at all three farms tomorrow, and then concentrate on not more than two or three areas of management that seem basic, and which we can develop useful programs for, before moving on to other areas.'

Over the next two days Stella absorbed more information on the logistics of farming than she had ever known before in her entire life. She took notes, and wondered how Russ seemed to be able to contain it all in his head.

'I had a farming background,' he told her, when she expressed her doubts. 'I know the basics, and then I have the experience of the six months in Canada operating a farm computer, though the set-up is different there, of course, with the cattle locked in barns all winter with electronically controlled feed bins. But anyway, during the day I concentrate on listening to Warwick and the other farm managers and absorbing what they say. Then I write it all down at night while it's still fresh in my mind.'

'Well, I'm glad to hear you're not a superbrain after all,' she said dryly. 'Personally, I don't care if I never hear the words "feed budget" or "liveweight gain forecast" again!'

'But then you're only a poor little city girl,' he grinned. 'Where were you brought up?'

'In the country,' she retorted. 'Well, small country towns, anyway. My father was a teacher, and I spent most of my holidays with friends who lived on farms. When I was ten my ambition was to marry a farmer and spend my life among cows, sheep and horses.'

'Well, who would have thought it, to look at you now?'

'As you grow older,' she told him, 'you learn that it doesn't do to make hasty judgments. They're so often dead wrong.'

A gleam entered his narrowed eyes, and he looked down at her, rocking back a little on his heels, his hands thrust into his pockets. 'Yes, aren't they?' he murmured. 'For instance, I thought you'd be prepared to accept a person on his merits.'

'I do!'

'Then why do you continually feel a need to remind me of my less than great age?'

'Nonsense. I haven't——'

'Yes, you have,' he cut in ruthlessly. 'You never miss a chance.'

'Rubbish. Now you *are* being over-sensitive.'

'I've never been accused of it before.'

'There's a first time for everything, isn't there?'

Stella said sweetly and, turning away, left him while she went to talk to Marianne.

They went back to Auckland on the Sunday afternoon, accomplishing the journey home without stopping except to top up the petrol tank.

'Where do you live?' she asked Russ as they approached the city.

'Drop me anywhere on your route. I'll find my own way home.'

'Don't be silly,' Stella said crisply. 'Tell me the address and I'll take you there.'

'I've got a better idea. Drive us to your place, and when you've freshened up, I'll take you out to dinner. Which I will pay for. No expense accounts.'

'Oh, I don't think——'

'Why not?'

'Well, for one thing——'

'What? I'm an employee, and you don't dine out with the lower orders except on business, is that it?'

'No, of course not,' said Stella hastily.

'Of course it isn't that, or of course you don't?'

'Of course it isn't that!' she snapped. 'Don't put words into my mouth!'

'Well, you seem to have trouble getting them there yourself. You haven't appeared to hate my company this weekend.'

'Of course I don't hate your company.' Most of the time they had got on very well. Even the few moments of tension and disagreement had been oddly stimulating. 'But,' she added, 'I don't go out to dinner with everyone whose company I can tolerate.'

She saw his jaw tighten, and after a moment he said quietly, 'I see. I didn't intend to back you into a corner. Sorry.'

Stella's foot slackened on the accelerator. 'No, *I'm* sorry,' she said quickly. 'That was rude, and not even true. I've enjoyed the weekend. I'd like to have dinner with you——' She was going to add, *but*, and go on to refuse again, more tactfully, but as she hesitated, the truth of the statement hit her. She would like to accept his invitation, and there wasn't a single good reason why she shouldn't.

Russ waited, letting the words hang in the air before he said, 'Right, that's settled, then. Anywhere in particular you'd like to go?'

Stella shook her head, suddenly stupidly nervous. 'I'll leave it to you, but I'd prefer somewhere not too formal.'

When they reached the architect-designed house in the wealthy suburb of Remuera, which she had shared with Mark, she garaged the car, and Russ took her bag from the boot and followed her inside.

In the spacious entry hall she said, 'You can leave the bag here, thanks. Come into the lounge.'

He followed her and stood looking about him at the room they had entered. Powder blue walls and a dark blue carpet offset each other and were augmented by paintings in gilt frames. Deep chairs in soft pastel blue leather were grouped about a large coffee table which was a single sheet of smoked glass held on the great curved horns of a brass antelope head, and in one corner was a pile of gold velvet floor cushions with heavy gold rope piping finished with tassels.

'Who decorated this room?' asked Russ.

'Mark chose the colours and some of the furniture,' she said, motioning him to sit down. 'The final touches were added by me.'

'It's a perfect foil for you,' he said. 'Not only the colours, but the mood. Cool and yet soft, and with a touch of the unexpected. He must have loved you very much.'

Again he had caught her unawares with a

surprisingly personal remark. Her voice not quite steady, she said, 'I loved him, too.'

He was standing in front of one of the chairs, but had not sat down. He looked at her across the few yards that separated them, with that disconcertingly direct look that made her feel that he was trying to see inside her head. Then he nodded silently as though verifying what she had told him, and sat down.

'Would you like a drink?' she asked him, crossing the room to a cabinet on the opposite wall.

'No, thanks.'

She stopped and turned uncertainly to face him.

'I don't want a drink just now,' he said. 'But don't let me stop you.'

'No,' she said. 'I don't drink much. I think I'll go and unpack and have a shower. Unless you'd like a cup of tea or something?'

'No, I don't need anything. I'll take your bag to your room, though.'

He stood up, and Stella quelled an impulse to refuse the offer as he made his way to the hall. She led him down the passageway to her bedroom, a small room furnished in cream and gold, a thick white rug almost covering the fitted carpet, a cream crocheted spread on the single bed.

Russ glanced about, placed the bag at the foot of the bed, and left without comment.

She unpacked and then had a quick shower and changed into a soft mauve crêpe dress with a draped neckline, redid her hair and applied light make-up.

When she went into the lounge she found Russ standing by the bookshelf under the window, leafing through a book on New Zealand trees that Mark had given her. She wondered if he had seen the inscription—*To my darling wife, with all my love Mark*—on the flyleaf.

He looked up as she came in, and said, 'You're beautiful.'

The book was still open in his hands, and the admiration in his eyes created in her a peculiar feeling of breathlessness. 'Thank you,' she said somewhat stiltedly. 'If you'd like to use the bathroom, please do so. You may want to change.'

'I will put on a clean shirt, if you don't mind,' he said, sliding the book back among the others. 'I won't be long.'

'It's next door to my room,' she told him. As he went out, she sank down in a chair and clasped her hands tightly together, noting the dampness of her palms. She heard him come in, and the bathroom door closed. She had a sudden picture of him in the swimming pool, his hair slicked down and his face streaming with water, and his nearly naked body perfectly proportioned, broad shoulders tapering to narrow waist, and hips and long, lean, muscled legs.

At the time she had scarcely noticed, and yet now she recalled clearly that his chest was lightly tanned and smooth except for a sprinkling of dark, wiry hair disappearing in a vee into the top of his swim shorts.

She shook her head and stood up to go to the window. This was crazy. She couldn't be sexually attracted to a man young enough—young enough for what? A few years younger than herself, that was all.

But certainly old enough to make her aware of him as a man. And she couldn't afford to be. It was too ridiculous. He was not only several years younger than she, he was an employee of the firm, and handsome and charming enough to have plenty of young girls his own age and younger to choose from. He might have invited her out to dinner, but that was probably simply because, like her, he didn't relish the thought of an evening alone to finish off an enjoyable weekend. It would have been too flat. And it had been a bit late to contact some other, younger and more desirable girl to share his evening with. And—with a chill the unwelcome thought insidiously entered her mind—he was an ambitious young man; taking the boss to dinner, paying her a compliment or two, might not do his career any harm.

They went to a small quiet restaurant where the food was good and the service excellent. Stella, remembering the hearty farm lunch of cold meat, potato and green salads which Marianne had served before they left, opted for a salmon entrée with a mushroom omelette and side salad to follow, but for himself Russ ordered marinated chicken wings and a carpetbag steak with vegetables, with a Black Forest Gâteau for dessert.

Watching him attack the main course with relish, Stella couldn't help smiling, though she refrained from comment. Looking up, he caught her eye and she had a feeling he was reading her thoughts. He shrugged, picked up his wineglass and silently lifted it to her, his eyes knowing, his expression ruefully resigned.

'I didn't say a thing!' she protested.

'No, but your face is saying it for you. Didn't your husband have a good appetite?'

'Actually, yes. But he didn't eat with such obvious enjoyment.'

'Is that a polite way of calling me a pig?'

'No. Actually it's rather—rather refreshing.'

'Well, thanks. I'm glad you enjoy my youthful enthusiasm.'

'You're doing it again!'

'What?'

'Putting words in my mouth,' she said. 'I wish you wouldn't.'

Russ looked at her consideringly, then nodded. 'Right, I won't do it again. But I wish you'd stop looking at me as though you're my favourite aunt taking me out for a birthday treat.'

'I'm not!'

'Yes, you are. And you don't know how dangerous it is.'

'Dangerous?'

He tipped his head to one side for just a moment, his eyes keen, as though debating whether to say what was in his mind. Then deliberately he answered. 'It's becoming more and more tempting to do something drastic to make you take me seriously.'

'I do take you seriously. I think you're a brilliant y——a brilliant man, with a great future, and in case you weren't aware of it, it was largely due to my taking your qualifications seriously that you got the job of Project Manager.'

'I was aware of it,' he said. 'And I'm grateful, but that isn't what I meant, and you know it.'

Suddenly wary, Stella shook her head. 'I'm sorry, I didn't know it. I have no idea what you're talking about.'

'Oh, come on!' he said with soft disbelief. 'You're not an inexperienced girl—you're a woman, and beautiful with it. You must know when a man finds you attractive.'

She thought, it seems that I'm not very good at picking it. First Owen, then Gavin, and now you. Aloud she said, 'Don't be silly, Russ.'

His closed fist thudded softly on to the tablecloth. 'Sometimes I could shake you!'

'Violence doesn't solve anything.'

'I don't know. I might just wake you up.'

'I don't need waking up, thank you,' she said coldly.

'That's a matter of opinion.'

What had June said about Gavin deciding to wake her up? It seemed all the men she knew had some sort of picture of her as the Sleeping Beauty, and themselves as the handsome prince whose destiny was to wake her.

Putting down her fork, she said, 'Perhaps having dinner together was a mistake. We've seen too much of each other this weekend.'

'It wasn't a mistake. Eat your omelette.' Russ sawed viciously at the steak on his plate, although the meat was tender and succulent. 'What's so terrible about us developing a personal relationship?'

Were they? She could hardly deny it. Somehow this weekend they had moved from a business plane to at times a very personal one.

'I don't think it's a good idea to mix business and—and social life,' she said.

'I don't believe that,' he said flatly. 'I know you've had dinner with Owen Armstrong at least once since I've been at Rawson's. And your secretary told me you often have a meal at their place, that you're godmother to one of her kids. And what about Gavin Jepson?'

She glanced up and saw him looking at her keenly, his eyes sharp on her face. 'What about him?' she asked warily.

'Is he special?'

'Why should you think he's special?' she parried.

'You know why. You don't play Sleeping Beauty with him, do you?' he added, giving her an uncanny feeling that he had read her thoughts. 'He's the lucky guy who gets to kiss the princess.'

About to hotly deny that he had done so with her permission, Stella paused. 'My relationship with Gavin is nothing to do with you,' she said.

'Fair enough. But it proves my point. You don't really object to mixing with business associates—even the ones on a lower scale—in a social way, you're not that much of a snob. So why pretend with me? Am I trespassing on Gavin Jepson's territory?'

He was waiting for an answer, and at last she said, 'No. I'm not—involved with Gavin.'

'With anyone?'

'Look, this is none of——'

'Is there anyone?' he cut in.

'No, but——'

'Good.'

He returned to his meal, apparently satisfied, and Stella sat indignantly watching him take a mouthful and swallow it before she found her voice. 'That doesn't mean,' she said at last, 'that I have any intention of being involved with you!'

He looked up, and gave her a smile of great charm. 'I know,' he said, and picked up his wine, his eyes laughing at her over the rim as he drank. 'Eat your omelette,' he repeated as he replaced the glass on the table. 'It's getting cold.'

Defeated, she obeyed. When they talked again, it was about neutral topics—the McLeod farms, the tension in the Middle East, and a recent New Zealand film that was breaking box office records on the home market and seemed destined to do well overseas.

She refused a sweet again, and the waiter brought Russ's gâteau, rich and dark with chocolate, topped with a good two inches of thick whipped cream and decorated with cherries.

He scooped up a spoonful and offered it to her. 'Have a taste?'

Stella hesitated, then leaned forward slightly and allowed him to spoon it into her mouth. It was delicious, moist and mouthwatering.

'Sure you won't change your mind?' he asked her.

'No, that's enough.'

He shrugged, and turned his attention to the dish before him.

'You'll get fat,' she warned.

He grinned. 'Well, if I do, I'll enjoy myself on the way!'

She couldn't really see him getting fat. He seemed extremely fit, and all the walking over hills they had done during the weekend hadn't even made him slightly short of breath.

'Do you play any sports?' she asked him.

He nodded. 'Tennis and squash.'

'No team sports?'

'Not my style. I hated football at school. I used to dream up all kinds of excuses not to play. What about you?'

'I like tennis,' she said. 'And I've played a bit of badminton. I used to be goalie in the school netball team once, but that was a long time ago.'

'Of course,' he mocked her. 'In the dim, dark days of your youth.'

'That's right,' she agreed blandly, meeting his eyes.

His mouth quirked up, and he said softly, as he pushed away the sweet dish, 'You're asking for it.'

Her heart skipped a beat. 'What?'

'You'll see. Coffee?'

They lingered over the coffee, talking in a desultory fashion, and Stella discovered that she had no desire for the evening to end. In spite of clashing with Russ once or twice, she had enjoyed herself, and again she realised that although he was often an uncomfortable companion, he was also a stimulating one. She didn't remember feeling so alive since Mark had gone.

Was that it? It was only recently that she had begun to be able to think and speak of Mark without pain. She was getting over it, her grief healing at last. Perhaps this disturbing awareness of another man was part of the process, part of coming to life again after a period of a terrible, grey dullness when she had clung desperately to the lifeline of Rawson Electronics in order to keep going somehow through the fog of grief, and hoped that some day she would emerge from it into the light of a new day, and a new reason for living. She had deliberately made the firm that reason, regarding it as an obligation to her husband, a memorial to him as well as a healing therapy for herself. But now she had mastered the running of the business, and increasingly was becoming aware that it was not enough. Strangely, having overcome the mourning period, she was more conscious than ever of the vast gap which Mark's passing had left in her life.

Perhaps this was just a new symptom of returning to normality, the ability to experience sexual attraction manifesting itself simply because the time was right and the man happened to be there, young, attractive, virile. A temptation, but one she must resist. She had no intention of making a fool of herself over Russ Langford.

He had insisted on getting a taxi to take them to the restaurant, and he ordered another afterwards. When it drew up outside the house, she was relieved to hear him tell the driver to wait for him before following her up the path to the darkened porch, hung with yellow jasmine that scented the cool night air.

She fitted her key in the lock and pushed at the door, then turned to thank him.

'I hope you enjoyed it,' he said, and for a moment his head blotted out the street lamp behind him as he bent and brushed her lips with his.

It was a light, fleeting kiss, and Stella was stunned at the electric tingle which passed through her. She drew back quickly, her fingers involuntarily flying to her mouth, touching where his lips had touched.

'Goodnight,' she said in a muffled voice, and turned blindly to go inside.

She heard him make some low exclamation, then he

pushed he door wider and stepped into the hall behind her. His hand fastened on her wrist, bringing her firmly towards him, and even as she made a small protesting sound, his arms went round her waist, and his mouth found hers again, firmly this time, brooking no denial, in a kiss that was hard, passionate and very adult.

Her hand went automatically to his shoulders, meaning to repulse him, but somehow lingering instead, caressing his upper arms under the thin shirt he wore, and then moving over his shoulder blades and until her fingers found his neck and thrust into his hair. His mouth was exploring hers, and she answered every movement of his lips, her head tipped back, her body straining against his.

But when he brought his hands down, pressing her to him, letting her feel his arousal, she suddenly broke the kiss, turning her head from him and struggling against his hands.

She found herself pinned against the wall near the door, Russ's hands running upwards over her stomach and waist to her breasts, staying there possessively, making flame leap through her body.

His mouth sliding to her neck, he whispered, 'Stella——'

'No,' she said raggedly. 'No—please. Stop, Russ!'

He lifted his head, and in the darkness his eyes seemed to glow. His hands came up to her face, and he said her name again.

'Your taxi's waiting,' she said desperately, her hands palms flat on the wall behind her.

'I could send it away.'

'No!'

She could feel the rise and fall of his chest, hear his breathing. Finally he sighed deeply, and his hands left her.

'Okay,' he said. 'Goodnight, Stella.'

He shut the door behind him as he left, and moments later she heard the taxi drive away. She stayed where she was until her breathing steadied and the night stopped pulsating about her.

CHAPTER FIVE

'MR ARMSTRONG would like to talk to you,' her secretary told her the next morning as she entered the office.

'I'll go along and see him,' Stella said. 'Get on the phone and tell him to expect me in fifteen minutes, would you? And then you can bring the mail in if it's ready.'

'There isn't much,' said June a few minutes later as she she deposited the opened letters on the desk. 'Did you have a nice weekend?'

'Mm, not bad for a business weekend.' Stella reached for the first letter. 'I took some notes that I'd like typed up. Think you can do that today?'

'Yes, of course. I have the Symonds lease contract to do first, though. You wanted that as soon as possible.'

'Oh, yes—I'd forgotten.'

June blinked exaggeratedly. 'Forgotten? After all the effort you put into securing it?'

'Only for a moment,' said Stella. 'I'm not losing my grip.'

'I didn't think so for a minute.'

The phone on Stella's desk buzzed, and June looked at her enquiringly.

'I'll take it.' Stella picked up the receiver. Russ's voice said in her ear,' 'Stella? Can we talk?'

'No,' she said. 'Not just now.'

'Well, when——'

'I've got a very busy morning,' she said crisply, 'and Owen is expecting me in a few minutes. June will be typing up my notes on the Tarahanga project some time today, and I'll see that you get a copy in case they may be useful. If there's any problem connected with that——'

'No,' he said impatiently, 'no problems there, but——'

'Good. Then I suggest you get on with starting to work out a plan for Warwick, and perhaps draw up some preliminary designs for a hardware and software configuration that will fit his circumstances.'

'I can do that standing on my head. Stella——'

'That's hardly necessary,' she said in dry tones. 'Perhaps you'd like to get back to me when you have some concrete suggestions to show me.'

'I want to see you now, Stella——'

'As I said, I'm tied up today. And since it isn't urgent, let me know when you have a proposal drawn up.'

She hung up and June commented, 'You're a ball of fire this morning, aren't you? Was that Mr Langford?'

'Yes. Why?'

'I forgot to tell you, he was waiting at the door when I arrived, to see you, he said. But someone from his department called him away before you came. I asked him if I could give you a message, but he said no, no message.'

'Okay. It wasn't important.'

'Still, I wouldn't mind seeing the dishy Mr Langford any time, important or not,' mused the secretary.

Stella looked up from the mail. 'Really, June! And you a married woman! What would Vincent say?'

June grinned. 'There's no harm in looking, is there? Anyway, he's too young for me—unfortunately. You, too, I suppose.'

'Yes. Now, shall we get on with these letters? Will you write to this firm and enclose some pamphlets on the Gemini range, and offer them a demonstration? Find out when Noelle will be free to conduct it . . .'

Just fifteen minutes later she entered Owen's office, and experienced a familiar qualm of unease as his eyes lit up at the sight of her. So far he had not followed up the hint he had given her about his feelings, and Stella had tried to maintain an air of detached friendship when she was with him.

'You wanted to see me, Owen?'

'Yes, sit down.' He came round the desk to place a chair for her quite unnecessarily, and hovered there, making her shift nervously in the seat, before he went back behind the desk.

For a few moments he just sat there, staring down at his blotter in its leather holder, and Stella said patiently, 'What was it you wanted to see me about, Owen?'

He seemed to start, and began rummaging in a drawer. 'Well, the cost analysis on the new extensions to the workroom,' he said, and drew out a folder which he opened and began to take papers from to show her. 'Here's the building plan, and the builder's estimate . . .'

Relieved, Stella hitched her chair forward and listened. Owen would discourse happily for hours once he had some figures in front of him and the chance to explain them.

But when they had finished the discussion, and she made to pass him one of the papers to return to the folder, he suddenly snatched at her hand, saying urgently, 'Stella!'

She raised startled eyes to his face, and caught her breath in dismay.

He began to speak again, but she forestalled him swiftly. 'Owen, before you say anything—I love you dearly as a friend, and I'd hate anything to spoil that. I value your friendship a great deal.'

He looked down at her hand in his and loosened his grip, and she turned hers to clasp his lightly, resting on the desk between them.

'You mean that you'd never think of me as anything closer than a friend, don't you?' he asked her.

'Yes.'

He shook his head dejectedly, looking down at their joined hands. 'Well, I was pretty sure you'd feel like that. You could have your pick, and I'm just a dull old accountant.'

'Owen, you're nothing of the kind! You're a very generous, clever, kindhearted man, and you deserve someone far better than me. I hope you find her.'

He removed his fingers from hers and gave her hand a little pat. 'That's kind of you, my dear. But I don't somehow think there'll be anyone else for me. I suppose it was asking too much of life to give me a second chance at the kind of happiness I had with Molly. Perhaps I should be content with my memories. It's just that sometimes life gets very lonely.'

'I know,' she said softly. 'It does.'

He looked up at her. 'You're too young to keep on feeling like that, though,' he said. 'I hope there will be someone for you, soon. Mark would have wanted you to be happy, I'm sure.'

'Yes, I know. But I don't think there's anyone who could replace him.'

'Well, I wasn't expecting to do that, you know. Only I thought maybe you could have loved me a little—in a different way. I'm a lot older than you, of course.'

'Only a year or two older than Mark was,' she said swiftly.

'Yes. That's one reason I thought—well, never mind. Post-mortems are grisly affairs, aren't they? I value your friendship too, Stella. Let's not allow this to alter that.'

'Of course not.' She smiled at him warmly, trying to ignore the hurt look in his eyes, and hoping that in time he would be able to do more than simply put a brave face on it as he was doing now. Surely, after all the years he had known her, this had been only a temporary aberration and they could return to their old footing with a minimum of heartache.

But the incident left her feeling sensitive and rather saddened. She wished she had been able to return Owen's feelings. It would have been nice to spend the rest of her life with someone so sweet-natured, understanding and gentle. Nice, but ... something would certainly have been missing, the extra something that she had shared with Mark, the delicious excitement of being in love.

Passing one of the demonstration rooms on the way back to her own office, she ran into Gavin Jepson. He came out of the room unexpectedly, and she was brought up short by the sight of his bulky frame, almost cannoning into him.

He put out a hand to steady her and kept his fingers on her arm, firmly enough so that she would have had to make a point of drawing away. 'Well, this is a pleasant surprise,' he drawled. 'June said you were busy with Owen.'

'I was,' she said shortly. 'Did you want me for something?'

He laughed very softly. 'Now, that's a leading question. You know I always want you, Stella.'

Trying to ease her arm out of his hold, she said, 'I'm sure that's very flattering, Gavin, but I happen to be busy——'

'Oh, come on, Stella, you're not that busy. Anyway, I want some advice. Come in here.'

He still had hold of her arm, and unwillingly she

allowed him to lead her into the room, where one of their newest word processors stood on a table, its screen blank.

'One of the girls was going to show me how it works, but she got called away,' he said. 'I thought I could use one of these in the office.'

'I expect you could,' she said, at last freeing her arm, and walking over to the screen. 'Or your secretary could. You know the basic functions of a word processor. All of them are computers programmed to function as very fancy typewriters.'

'Yes, but this particular model is one I haven't seen before. I'm told it combines the functions of a calculater within the word processing function, so that you don't have to change disks or even return to the menu of different functions on a disk to carry out a calculating task in the middle of a letter or report.'

'Yes, that's right. It has a very easy switchover from word processing mode to calculating mode, and it can be done without removing the existing data from the screen.'

'Show me,' he suggested.

'Gavin, I'm not a demonstrator——'

'I know. But you have a play with every machine that comes into the building, and you've a basic working knowledge of each one. I remember you telling me that you figured it's part of the job to know the basics. Just give me a quick demo of how this calculating mode goes, will you? Please.'

Stella had made the mistake of standing by the machine on its table, enabling him to get between her and the door, so that it wasn't easy to just say sorry and walk out past him.

She shrugged, sat down at the operator's chair and switched on the machine.

The screen mounted above the typewriter-style keyboard lit up, and a message appeared on it asking for insertion of a disk. She found the pre-programmed disk and inserted it in one of the two slots in the disk drive section of the machine beside the screen, and then slid an unused blank disk, which would store new data typed into the machine, into the other slot, and pressed a key on the keyboard. Another 'prompt' message appearing on screen, she typed in the date and her name, and the machine presented a backlit screen, with a status line indicating in green lettering how many line and letter spaces were available.

Gavin was standing behind her chair, and she felt him put his hands lightly on her shoulders.

Quickly she typed a few lines of a standard business letter, which appeared on the screen, then asked by a series of keystrokes for 'calculator mode' and typed in some quite complicated arithmetical problems, which the computer solved on request, then returned to 'word mode' to finish off the letter with 'Yours faithfully.'

Gavin's fingers were caressing her neck, and as she instructed the machine to close down so that she could remove the disks, she said, 'Please don't do that.'

'Do what?' he asked lazily, his fingers slipping insidiously inside her neckline.

'You know perfectly well what!' she snapped, taking the disks out of the drive. 'Please stop touching me.'

He moved away as she got up, and stood looked at her as she said, 'There you are, you've had your demonstration. Satisfied?'

'Far from it, darling. How about I give you a demonstration, hmm?'

As he came towards her Stella stepped back, but the table was behind her, and although she raised her hands to ward him off, he was much too strong and determined for her resistance to be effective. He held her and kissed her, and she went rigid, then pushed against him furiously.

Her anger had no effect except to make him force her lips apart rather brutally, his hand pulling at her hair, his mouth so hard and determined that he hurt her, pressing her inner lip sharply against her teeth, and she actually became afraid of what he might do. She kicked, and tried to bite, and he released her at last, muttering with astonished fury, 'You bitch!'

'*Don't you ever touch me again!*' Stella grated between clenched teeth, closing her hands at her sides in an effort to maintain some semblance of calm when she wanted to claw at him, or at the very least slap his arrogant face.

'You don't mean that——' he said ingratiatingly, making a remarkably swift recovery.

'I mean it,' she said, her voice throbbing with fury. 'I mean every word of it. If you *ever* lay one *finger* on me again, I'll get you thrown off the board, and I'll tell them exactly why!'

He laughed incredulously. 'You don't suppose the board will ask for my resignation, simply on account of a stolen kiss or two? You're crazy? You can't——'

'And you're crazy if you think I'll put up with this kind of harassment from you or anyone else. Keep your hands *off* or you'll find out just what I *can* do!'

'It's your pretty boy, isn't it?' he jeered insolently as she turned on her heel. 'You're getting it from him, are you?'

Her mouth thinned ominously, but she ignored him. She wouldn't dignify his petulant reprisal with a reply. She stalked out of the room and went swiftly along the corridor, her cheeks flushed with anger, her arms rigidly at her sides.

She turned a corner and saw Russ coming out of a doorway, and made to pass him without a glance. Right now she didn't want to see anyone—particularly any man—particularly him.

'Stella,' he said as she passed. Then, as she ignored

him, he caught at her arm, his fingers warm and hard. 'Stella!'

She didn't think. She just reacted, her hand opening and swinging in a wide arc and connecting with his cheek in a stinging slap as she ground out, 'Don't *touch* me! I've had enough of being *manhandled*!'

For a moment the mark on his cheek stood out, before he flushed darkly and stepped back from her. His eyes glittering, he snapped furiously, 'And *I've* had enough of being treated like the office boy!'

He turned his back and and went back into the room he had left and shut the door.

Stella stared at it blankly for a moment and then went on. She didn't remember going past June and into her office, but a few minutes later she was sitting at her desk, looking at the wall and vaguely aware that her palm was stinging.

'She lifted it and stared at the reddened skin, then put her head in her hands, closing her eyes.

June came in, saying, 'Are you all right?'

Stella lifted her head, smiling wanly. 'I'm okay. I just did something I shouldn't have.'

'Well, don't we all? Does it matter?'

'I—think it does. Do you need me just now?'

'If you'll just sign these, I can get them into the post before lunch.'

Stella signed, her mind not on what she was doing. 'I'm going to see Russ Langford for a few minutes,' she said, 'but try not to disturb us, would you?'

'Sure. You don't want me to ask him to come to you?'

'Not this time, June. I—think I need to see him in his own office.'

When she knocked on his door he called, 'Come in,' but he was not alone. Two other staff members were with him, poring over a chart that he had spread out on his desk.

Stella saw the surprise in his eyes, followed by a cold blankness as he straightened. 'Mrs Rawson,' he said formally. Then, 'I'm rather busy at the moment—is it urgent?'

She caught a glimpse of the other men's faces registering discreetly hidden astonishment, but she wasn't looking at them. Her eyes on Russ, her cheeks faintly stained with colour, she said evenly, 'Yes, it is.' And waited.

He nodded dismissal, but the others were already moving towards the doors. She stood aside to let them pass, then closed it behind them and leaned on the panels.

'I came to apologise,' she said. 'I had no right to hit you. And it—it wasn't really aimed at you, anyway.'

'I thought your aim was pretty good, actually,' he said, touching his cheek. 'But,' he came round the desk and stood watching her, his gaze darkly inimical, 'I don't recall that you complained about being *manhandled* last night. You were a bit late with your reaction, weren't you?'

'You don't understand,' she said, 'I was—I was referring to someone else. And it was him that I should have—would have liked to—slap in the face. You just happened to get in the way at the wrong time. I'm sorry.'

His face began to lose its taut look. 'I begin to see,' he said slowly, then frowning, added, '*Owen?*'

The idea was so unlikely that she laughed. 'Good heavens, no!' she said.

'Well, I thought you'd just been with him. You said you had to see him, and when I tried to catch you in your office, June said that's where you were.'

'I ran into—someone else on the way back,' Stella explained.

'Tell me who he is and I'll punch his nose for him.'

Stella smiled very faintly. 'Thanks for the offer, but I'd rather you didn't.'

His eyes searched her face. Grimly he said, 'I think I can guess, anyway. Did he hurt you in any way?'

She flushed. 'No. I don't want to talk about it, Russ. I'd better get back.'

She turned to go, but his hand reached the door handle first. He didn't open it, but stayed there, his eyes inspecting her face. 'You didn't slap my face last night,' he said softly. 'You didn't want to, did you?'

She couldn't meet his eyes. 'That's something else I don't want to talk about,' she said, 'Please forget it, Russ.'

'Forget it? *No*, I don't think so. I dreamed about it all night.'

Again a soft, tingling excitement attacked her. 'Don't?' she said. 'It happened. It's over. I shouldn't have let you——'

'It isn't over,' he insisted. 'Why say that? It could be just the beginning.'

Vehemently Stella shook her head. 'No, Russ. We both got a little carried away, but don't start building fantasies on it. There's no more to be said.'

Stubbornly he said, 'I think there is.'

'No! Open the door.' She lifted her head and looked at him haughtily, making it clear that she was giving him an order.

For a moment she thought he would refuse, then his mouth tightened and he turned the handle and swung the door open. She felt his eyes following her as she made her way along the passage back to her office.

CHAPTER SIX

SHE should have known that Russ wouldn't let it end there. A man with his ability to go after what he wanted and get it wouldn't give up that easily.

Yet when she answered the doorbell at home that evening, she was surprised to find him on the doorstep, looking handsome and determined, and dressed casually in jeans and a tee-shirt that made him appear even younger than when he wore business clothes.

'If it's business, Russ,' she said, 'can't it wait until morning?'

'It's not business. That's why I've waited until now.'

'Then I'm afraid——'

'Yes, I know. What of? I'm not going to rape you.'

'That isn't what I meant. Go away, Russ.'

He looked down at her, his eyes holding hers. 'All right,' he said quietly. 'If that's what you really want. But if I do, Stella, I go for good. So don't think you can just crook your finger and whistle me back if you change your mind. At work I have to dance to your tune, that's what I'm paid to do. After hours you don't pull the strings any more.' He paused. 'Now tell me again. Do I go?'

She hesitated just too long, knowing she should say the words, but finding them blocked by a sinking feeling of acute depression and a sense of burning boats that she didn't want to lose.

Russ put his hand on the edge of the door and pushed, quite gently. 'Okay,' he said. 'So let me in, Stella.'

Dumbly, she stood back and watched him come in and shut the door behind him.

'Don't look so scared,' he chided. 'I'm not going to take advantage of you just because you invited me in.'

'I didn't,' she pointed out.

'But you didn't stop me.'

'Could I have?' she retorted, beginning to rally.

'With a word. But you didn't say it. Can't we go and sit down?'

She gestured silently in the direction of the lounge, but he waited for her to precede him.

Nervously, Stella sat in one of the chairs, her back straight and her hands clasped in her lap.

Russ didn't sit down, but stood looking at her, one hand hooked into the belt loop of his jeans. 'Will you let me get you a drink?' he asked.

She wondered if she looked in need of one. 'Yes, please. Get one for yourself, too.' At least it would give her something to do with her hands. 'I'll have a dry sherry.'

He poured the drinks and brought hers over before seating himself opposite her, leaning back on the blue upholstery. 'Don't you ever wear your hair down?' he asked abruptly.

She had changed into a simple shift-style dress with a tie belt when she came home from the office, stripped off her tights and replaced her high-heeled pumps with flat-soled, thonged sandals, but her hair was still pinned in its neat, elegant knot.

Another personal question. She experienced a flutter of panic, wondering what she had got herself into. 'Only in bed,' she said quickly, and could have bitten her tongue. Hastily she sipped at the sherry, waiting for him to take her up on that remark.

But he didn't. He said, 'It must be pretty, down.'

Stella shook her head. 'I'm too old to wear it like that.'

He made a derisive sound. 'That's nonsense. Plenty of women older than you wear their hair loose.' He paused. 'Did your husband like you to look older?'

Surprised, she asked, 'Why should you think that?'

'I just wondered. He was so many years your senior, after all . . .'

'He liked me to look—sophisticated. It isn't quite the same thing.'

He nodded, and lifted his glass to his lips. 'Would you take your hair down for me?' he asked her.

'No,' she said sharply, and Russ smiled a little.

'Okay,' he said equably. 'Later.'

Alarm bells were ringing in her head suddenly. 'Look, just because I didn't send you away——'

'I know,' he said. 'Don't take too much for granted. All right, I won't.' He smiled at her, and unconsciously she relaxed, sitting further back in her chair.

'I like this room,' he said. 'I like sitting here like this, with you. It's—restful.'

He sighed and stretched out his long legs on the octagonal Persian rug between their chairs, closing his eyes.

Amused in spite of herself, Stella said, 'I hope you're not intending to sleep here.'

He opened his eyes, and she saw they were filled with laughter, and again all the connotations of her innocent remark flashed into her mind.

'Can't I?' he asked plaintively, his mouth curving into a teasing smile.

She shook her head, laughing back at him, suddenly lighthearted. He was a perfectly charming young man, and fun to be with, and he found her attractive. Why shouldn't she enjoy his company and let the future take care of itself?

He left quite early, taking her hand in his on the doorstep and unexpectedly lifting it to his lips to drop

a kiss on her palm. She heard him whistling softly as
he went down the path.

He called in again a few nights after that, and stayed
later, because they began talking about books when he
picked up a library choice of hers, and got caught up
in a discussion on the relative merits of their favourite
authors.

'What are you doing at the weekend?' he asked her
before he went.

'Nothing.'

'My sister's husband has been transferred to
Dunedin. They have a house on Waiheke that's up for
sale, and they've asked me to keep an eye on it. I
thought of spending the weekend there. Would you
like to come along?'

As she hesitated, he added patiently, 'I'm not
planning a big seduction scene. There are three
bedrooms and you can take your pick. It's not far from
Palm Beach, and there isn't much summer left. You'll
like it.'

She would, too, she thought. She had been to the
island twice on day trips, and had enjoyed the sunlit
beaches and the illusion of being away from it all,
although Auckland was less than a couple of hours
across the water by ferry boat. It would be pleasant to
spend the weekend soaking up sun before the summer
ended.

'All right,' she said. 'I'll come.'

The house was perched above the beach, looking
down on the Pacific waves rolling into a broad strip of
sand bounded by black rock outcrops. As Russ had
promised, there were three bedrooms, one large one
with a double bed, and two with two singles each. The
beds were stripped, but Russ found sheets and
blankets for them in a cupboard.

'They took their favourite things with them, but left the basic furniture to be sold with the house,' he explained, as he handed her two of the sheets. 'And Lorraine promised to leave a few sheets and towels behind so that I wouldn't have to bring them every time I came over. Which room do you want?'

'I don't know. Do you have any preference?'

'Take the one with violets on the wallpaper,' he suggested. 'It was Sally's room. I'll be next door.'

Both the smaller rooms and the living room opened with glass sliding doors on to a broad terrace facing the sea. When Stella had made up the bed, and unpacked a few things, she opened the door and went to lean on the wooden railing and admire the view.

When Russ joined her, she smiled at him, her gaze curious. 'So you're an uncle,' she said.

He rested his forearms on the railing, and turned his head to smile quizzically back at her. 'You sound surprised.'

'I hadn't pictured it, that's all. Do you like children?'

'Some. I like Sally and Ned—that's her little brother. They're nice kids. I think Lorraine and Pete are doing a good job on them. Do *you* like kids?'

'Yes.' She straightened, and moved away. 'Will your sister have left any supplies in the kitchen? I could do with a cup of tea.'

'We'll look,' he said, following her through the living room door and into the kitchen. 'There won't be any milk, though.'

Russ opened a cupboard near the stove, saying, 'It used to be kept in here——' and withdrew a packet of tea bags and a screw top jar of sugar. '*Voilà!*'

'Good!' Stella reached out to take them from him, but he didn't relinquish his hold.

'Did I touch a sore spot just now?' he asked her quietly.

Her eyes met his fleetingly, and saw the concern in his face.

'It doesn't matter,' she said.

'Yes, it does. I don't want to hurt you.'

'I know.'

He released his hold, and let her take the tea and sugar to place on the work bench by the sink.

She put them down and said, 'I wanted to have children, but we decided to wait. And then—Mark died.'

She felt his hands on her shoulders, then he leaned down and kissed her cheek. It was over in a moment, and he had moved away from her to open another cupboard, but she felt extraordinarily comforted, the brief sharp regret that had been woken in her utterly dispelled.

'They've taken the electric jug,' he reported, 'but I've found a pot to boil water in. And some cups. Nothing to eat, though, I'm afraid. We'll need to go down to the corner store and lay in some supplies.'

'I'll settle for a cup of tea on its own just now.' She put the tea bags in the cups while he boiled the water, and found some spoons in a drawer. Everything had been provided for two, she noticed, and wondered if his sister had been expecting him to bring a girl here.

'Okay,' he said, lifting the pot from the stove. 'Ready?'

They sat at the bare pine table. Stella noticed he heaped three spoons of sugar into his, and winced. He grinned, and said, 'Usually I have it with milk and only one sugar.'

'Your teeth will fall out,' she warned him.

He laughed, so that she couldn't help noticing that his teeth were very nearly perfect. Like the rest of him, she thought. He really was too much. 'Yes, Mama,' he said, his eyes teasing wickedly, and she made a face at him.

'I'm not old enough to be your mother!'

'Well, I'm glad you admit it. I've been trying to convince you of that for months.'

'That isn't necessary.'

'It seems to me it's highly necessary. You'd think you were thirty years older than me, instead of three.'

'Four,' she corrected him automatically.

'Three,' he insisted. 'I've had a birthday.'

'Oh—I didn't know. When?'

He shrugged. 'A couple of weeks back.'

'Congratulations. I'll be thirty in a few months' time.'

'So? We're both getting older.'

'But I'm getting older faster.'

His brows went up comically, and he shook his head. 'What?'

'I mean—when you're older, you age faster——' She saw the look of exaggerated scepticism on his face and began to giggle like a schoolgirl. 'You know what I mean!'

He was laughing. 'You're crazy! Einstein should know about you.'

'That's what I mean!' Stella tried to explain, between giggles. 'It's to do with the theory of relativity.'

'Oh, yeah!' he said with mock sarcasm. 'Tell me all about it.'

It was hopeless. She had to give up, but when they had sobered and finished their tea, she reached over to touch his hand briefly. 'You're nice, Russ,' she said simply. 'I haven't laughed like that since Mark died. Thank you.'

For one instant his face went tautly expressionless. Then he smiled at her and turned his hand to clasp her fingers warmly. A moment later he released her and stood up. 'Come on, we'd better wash these up and get those supplies. Or better yet, we'll go down to the beach and get the supplies on our way back.'

They lazed on the beach for the rest of the day, only moving to walk to the store for ice creams and a packet of crisps when they felt peckish, and to wade into the water for swims.

Lying prone after a dip, Stella started as she felt cold lotion splash on her back. Russ said, 'You're starting to burn. Keep still. Didn't you put some sunscreen on before we came down?'

'Yes, but it's probably washed off.' His hand was stroking softly over her back, spreading the lotion in rhythmic circles. Deft fingers unhooked the bra top of her swimsuit, and he said, 'You don't want a strap mark, do you?' He made a last sweeping movement from her nape to the top of her bikini pants, then he stopped touching her.

He probably did it for his girl-friends all the time, she told herself. He had certainly dealt very easily with that hook—not that it was a complicated one.

And she hadn't really wanted him to stop. Shamed, she lay still, her flaming cheeks hidden, her face pillowed on her arms. Thank goodness he couldn't know how he had made her feel!

Rationalising, she told herself that it was purely a physical reaction. No man had touched her so intimately since Mark died. Her body was at last awakening to dormant emotions, and it was naturally ready to respond to any touch.

No, not any touch, she admitted honestly. She had been touched before—gently, by Owen, and roughly, by Gavin Jepson. And before she had angered him into a brutal desire to hurt, Gavin had been kissing her with what she had to recognise as considerable skill—his technique had been quite startling. And yet she had felt nothing like the arousal that Russ had evoked with a touch of his fingertips.

He didn't seem to share her feelings, though. Cautiously she lifted her head slightly to look at him.

He was lying on his back, his arms at his side, perfectly relaxed and apparently dozing.

A tendril of hair blew across her eyes, and as she brushed it back she felt a dewing of sweat at her temples. Her hair was coming loose from its pins, although she had skewered it firmly before going in the water, and her make-up had long gone. She probably looked a fright anyway, she thought, hardly likely to stimulate the male imagination.

Late in the day they went back to the store and bought a large paper bag full of groceries. They heated a tin of baked beans and chopped up bacon in the one pot they had to cook in, and made toast under the griller of the stove, burning the edges. But the meal was one of the best she had ever tasted, and she put it down to the sea air and the hunger engendered by swimming and sunbathing.

They washed up together, then took some cushions off the sofa in the lounge out to the terrace and sat there talking, until the dark sky was littered with bright stars, and a wind off the moonlit sea made Stella shiver and rub at her goosepimpled arms.

'Want to go in?' Russ asked her.

'Mm, I s'pose so. What's the time?'

'Only nine-thirty. I found a Scrabble game under the bed in my room. Want to play?'

'Scrabble? I haven't played for years. I used to love it.'

'Right, I'll get the box.'

He brought it out, and they played at the kitchen table, discovering that there were no 'U's among the letters, and inventing new rules to get round the problem, and arguing like children over the legality of each other's words, with no dictionary to appeal to.

Stella finally won by defending heatedly the use of 'orotond', which she insisted was a legitimate word meaning roundness of speech, and Russ reluctantly conceded defeat, but said darkly that he would demand a return match if he found, when he could get hold of an Oxford, that the dictionary didn't list the word.

It was midnight before they went to bed, and Stella slept like a baby.

She was up early, though. Hearing Russ stirring in the kitchen at about seven, she got up and into a short robe, brushed her hair and hastily pinned it, and made a quick visit to the bathroom before going through to the kitchen.

Russ was standing at the stove with a towel wrapped round his waist, boiling water in the pot.

'If you're making tea, I'll have some, too,' she told him.

'If you'd waited I'd have brought it in to you.' He lifted the pot and poured the water into two cups on the bench, and brought them over to the table. 'I thought you said you wore your hair down in bed.'

'I do.'

He looked at the neat shining coil and said nothing, but passed her the sugar before sitting down opposite her. 'Thought I'd go for a swim,' he said, 'Want to come?'

She looked out at the cool, fresh morning and said, 'Not to swim. I'll come down to the beach, though.'

She changed into a skirt and cotton top, but Russ strolled down as he was, and on the beach took off the towel to reveal his dark fitted swim shorts. Watching him plunge into the water with its silken morning sheen, Stella couldn't help noticing what a good masculine body he had, the body of a man at the peak of his physical development.

She turned to wander along the sand near the water line, which was low this morning, revealing a pattern of long, twisted ribbons reaching up the beach where

the waves had spread a shallow veil before receding,
leaving tiny pebbles and a few shells in their wake.
The rocks were exposed, and every hollow held a pool
of pellucid water where hermit crabs scooped the sand
with thread-thin curved arms, and sea anemones with
green, orange or purple petals clung to the rock walls.
There were tiny blue starfish under overhanging lips
of rock hung with frilly seaweed fronds, and larger
ones moving slowly among the busy crabs and darting
little transparent fish.

Sitting on her heels, Stella was watching a pinkish
starfish with long arms crawling across the sandy floor
of a pool when Russ joined her. He had dried his hair
roughly and slung the towel about his neck. He
squatted down beside her and watched, too, silently
sharing her absorbed interest.

A wave, coming higher than the others, splashed
over the edge of the rocks and sprayed them with
foam. Startled, Stella almost lost her balance and,
putting out her hand, touched his still damp chest.

He put a hand on her arm, and they stood upright
together, her fingers still brushing his skin, his hand
strong and warm as he held her steady.

She saw something flare in his eyes, and her own
went guarded, her fingers curling as she moved away
from him.

'Shall we walk to the next bay?' he asked.

It was the bay where nude bathing was tacitly
accepted, and he had not suggested going there
yesterday, but now the beach was deserted, and she
nodded.

It was only a short walk before the curve of sand
gave way to rocks jutting out into the sea. The sun was
weakly climbing beyond the rocks, and as they
retraced their steps it surmounted the shadow and
warmed the sand under her feet.

Breakfast was boiled eggs, toast and marmalade, and

while Russ washed up, Stella put their sheets through the washing machine in the small laundry off the bathroom and hung them out to dry.

When she came back to the kitchen, Russ was just coming through from the front door. 'How would you like to see some more of the island?' he asked her.

'What do you mean?'

'The next-door-neighbour called in to say hello and offer us the use of a motor scooter if we'd like to explore. They have a holiday home just down the hill, and were quite friendly with my sister and Pete. I met them a couple of times when I stayed here before.'

'I've never been on a motor scooter,' Stella confessed.

'As you said once, there's a first time for everything. If we're going, it might be better soon. Later in the day it's going to get too hot.'

She was nervous at first on the scooter. The road seemed very close and it tore away under the wheels at an alarming speed, but once she got used to it and dared to open her eyes and loosen slightly her death-grip on Russ's shirt, she began to enjoy herself. The wind on her face was fresh, but Russ's body protected her from the worst of it, and with her arms about his waist she felt relatively safe.

Inland, the island was very much like any New Zealand farming area, rolling hills and unsealed roads, and livestock grazing in the paddocks. But every so often they would come over a rise and find themselves overlooking a magnificent sea view with a small island on the horizon, or gazing down a green and gentle valley to a tiny hidden cove where blue water lapped at a crescent of shimmering sand.

Russ had a map and was able to pinpoint some of the landmarks for her. Once when he stopped at the crest of a hill and they looked down into a pretty bush-fringed bay, he said, 'That's Honeymoon Bay. Nice and private, isn't it?'

It was, and beautiful, too, but it was one of many, some of them only reachable through private land. Later, though, they found a way to one of the almost invisible little beaches, and Russ parked the scooter while they walked to the water's edge and let the wavelets lap at their bare feet.

They stripped to the swimsuits under their clothes and played about in the water, racing and splashing each other, diving and then floating on the buoyant surface.

Coming out, they flung themselves down on towels on the sand to dry out. Lying on her back, Stella felt the sun beating on her closed eyelids and evaporating the droplets of salt water from her skin. The sea shushed and murmured, and gulls in the distance screeched into the bright air. She felt utterly content for the first time in two years, totally relaxed and happy.

She sighed, and Russ said, sounding drowsy. 'What's the matter?'

'Nothing. I'm—perfectly—all right,' she told him, her voice creamy with satisfaction.

'Good,' he said. 'I'm glad.' His hand found hers and held it, his fingers between hers.

She woke to a featherlight touch on her mouth, struggling out of the depths of sleep to a sudden delicious, tingling awareness.

The touch left her, and she opened her eyes to see Russ looking down at her, his expression totally serious and questioning.

Involuntarily her lips parted, invited, and as his mouth came back to hers, her hands slid up to his hair.

His mouth was gentle but insistent and his hand began to caress her, trailing along her arm, stroking her thigh, and moving up over her hip to her waist and back again.

Her hands slipped down to his shoulders, liking the feel of the warm, muscled flesh, and he shifted to bring himself closer, his body poised over her and then coming down, arching her against him with his arm behind her waist as they exchanged more of those long, sweet, drugging kisses.

The blood was singing in her ears, her arousal gaining momentum, slowly building. His hand came between them and found her breast, pushing aside the flimsy top she wore, and she closed her eyes tighter in ecstasy and moaned deep in her throat. Then she suddenly felt him stiffen and shudder, and he wrenched his mouth away from hers to bury his lips against her neck, holding her so tightly it hurt.

In quick understanding, she wound her arms about him, her hands flat against his back, then moving into his hair, smoothing the tousled strands until he lay still, his mouth still pressed against her skin.

'I'm sorry,' he said, his voice muffled.

'It's all right,' she said. 'It was as much my fault——'

He lifted his head and said, 'You can't help being beautiful. My God, you are——'

Stella smiled and shook her head. 'No.'

'Yes.' He kissed her lips, hard and briefly, then got up and turned his back on her to run into the water.

CHAPTER SEVEN

STELLA closed her eyes, willing her uneven breathing to steady itself, her heartbeat to stop racing, her heated blood to cool down.

When Russ came back, his body glistening as the water ran down his chest and his legs, she was sitting up hugging her knees, looking more or less composed.

'Do something for me,' he said abruptly.

Stella turned to look at him. 'What?' she asked, her voice husky.

'Let your hair loose.'

She stared back at him for some seconds, then slowly raised her hands and began taking out the pins, scattering them on the sand. He watched her, his eyes very dark and very intent.

Her hair was fine and straight, and it fell past her shoulders, the faint breeze lifting a few strands and dropping them back again. It blew a shining wisp across her mouth, and he reached out, brushing her lips with his fingers, and smoothed it back, his hand lingering for a moment against her neck. 'It's lovely,' he said. 'And you're not too old to wear it like that.' He smiled and added, 'In fact, just now you look about sixteen.'

'I'm not sixteen. That's why I don't wear my hair like this.'

'Most women prefer to look younger than their age.'

'I'm a businesswoman. If I went round looking like a teenager no one would take me seriously. I have enough problems just being female.'

'Is there so much prejudice—still?' he asked sceptically.

'Stella shrugged. 'Some. It doesn't help, I suppose, that I took over from my husband. A lot of people seemed to think I was only filling in until I could get some man to do the job for me.'

'Is that why you feel the need to assert your authority?'

There was a pause. 'I don't think I do that,' she said defensively.

'No?'

The question was pointed, and she said, 'No. Do you really feel that I—— throw my weight around?'

'Well,' Russ said slowly, 'I haven't noticed you doing it with anyone else, but with me you've certainly made sure I know who's boss.'

Stella picked up a handful of sand and let it trickle through her fingers. 'I suppose I have,' she admitted, 'but that's because——'

'Because?' he prompted her, as she paused.

'Well, someone suggested that I'd pressed for your appointment because I—liked your looks. I was probably over-compensating, trying to prove that it wasn't true. I was determined to keep you at arm's length.'

He said slowly, 'Well, you might have saved yourself the trouble. I've no intention of being kept at arm's length, and you may as well know it.'

She looked at him fleetingly and saw him smiling at her, but in his eyes there was a hint of challenge.

Avoiding it, she said, 'Shouldn't we be getting back? It's well past lunch time.'

'Perhaps we should,' he agreed, getting up and holding out his hand to her to pull her to feet. 'We can still have another swim after lunch and be in plenty of time to catch the boat.'

'I hear you went to Waiheke for the weekend,' June

greeted Stella on Monday morning, her eyes alight with curiosity.

Brought up short, Stella asked, 'How did you know?'

June smiled wryly. 'I might as well tell you, it's all over the building by now. Michelle from reception saw you—with Russ Langford. Was it supposed to be a secret?'

'No, not exactly, but I don't particularly want my private life discussed by every member of the staff.'

'Don't think you can stop it, honey. It was private, then? Not business?'

'It was a holiday,' Stella said. 'A very innocent weekend.'

'I'll tell them it was business,' June offered.

Stella smiled affectionately at her secretary. 'You can try,' she said dryly. 'I don't suppose it will make much difference.'

'You said it.' As Stella made to go into her own office, June said, 'Stella——'

'Yes?'

'I know it's none of my business, but I'm fond of you, and—well, you do know what you're doing, don't you?'

'I'm just taking each day as it comes,' said Stella with a touch of defiance. 'And as I said, it was a very innocent weekend.'

'Right. I won't say any more.'

But June was troubled, Stella knew. Her question had been a warning—not to take Russ too seriously, perhaps—not to make a fool of herself.

Later in the day Owen wandered into her office and sat fingering his tie, a wide one today with a violet sunburst design superimposed on silver and blue stripes, that clashed wonderfully with his mustard-coloured shirt and green tweed jacket.

Knowing he would come to the point eventually, Stella waited patiently while he started and abandoned several sentences dealing with the weather, the prospects of a devaluation of currency and its possible effect on their export division, and the latest hold-up in the construction of the new extension to the building.

Finally he said, apparently at random, 'Did you have a nice weekend?'

Fixing him with a bland stare, she said, 'Very pleasant, thank you.'

'Um,' he said, running a forefinger round his collar, not doing his tie any good at all. 'I—er—hear you went to Waiheke.'

'I gather everyone in the building has heard it,' she said. 'They've also heard that I was with Russ Langford.'

'Yes,' he said, looking relieved. 'June says it was business.'

'You know perfectly well that it wasn't business,' she said crisply. 'But I should hope you'd also know that it wasn't a—an illicit sexual adventure, either. We stayed in the same house, in separate rooms. We had a very nice time. We came home. And none of that is anybody's business but mine and Russ's.'

'No, of course no, but as an old friend——'

'Yes?'

He squirmed unhappily. 'Well, I hope you know what you're doing, that's all.'

'Have you been talking to June?' she asked suspiciously.

'Why?'

'She said nearly the same thing. Why shouldn't I know what I'm doing?'

'Well, the two of you are getting talked about, for one thing.'

'That's a nuisance, not a disaster. Talk hurts no one, and it'll soon die down.'

'And—I wouldn't want you to be hurt.'

'Thank you, Owen. But I'm a grown woman, you know. I can look after myself.'

'Maybe. But Mark married you when you were only nineteen. You hadn't much experience of men before that, and what chance have you had to gain any, married to Mark? I know you've never looked at anyone else, before or since his death, until now.' Owen paused and went on quite belligerently, for him, 'Russ Langford's an ambitious young man, and I don't want to see him using you as a stepping stone.'

Rather nettled, she said, 'Isn't it possible he's simply attracted to me?'

'Of course it is. I'm not saying he isn't. Just that it could be convenient to be attracted to the widow of Mark Rawson. You must be aware that you'd be a very tempting target for a youngster wanting to make his mark in electronics. You have money, influence, you practically own this firm. You're a very desirable matrimonial prospect.'

She couldn't deny that. Hurt and angry, she asked, 'Is that why you wanted to marry me, Owen?'

As soon as she said it, she regretted the impulse. His face closed, and she got up from the desk, and came round it to say, 'I didn't mean it—I know it wasn't that. But why should Russ be any less sincere?'

'No reason. Except he hasn't been here three months yet. I just don't want him to rush you into something you might regret.'

'He's not rushing me into anything, actually, and he hasn't even hinted at marriage—or anything like it. We're just friends.' Even as she said it, she recalled the passionate kisses they had exchanged on the beach, and deliberately brushed aside the memory. Kisses these days meant very little, anyway. She still wasn't sure if Russ had meant anything by them, and certainly a few kisses didn't constitute any sort of binding promise.

But after Owen had gone she found herself, in spite of her sensible reflections, thinking of what he had said. He had no malice in him, and would have been happy for her to find a man who could give her what Mark had given her, a happy and passionate marriage. Owen was a true friend, and he had tried to warn her to take care. A cold trickle of uncertainty began to dispel the sense of euphoria which had followed the weekend.

Stella skipped lunch, so didn't see Russ then. But just before five he came into her office, saying, 'Can I talk to you for a moment?'

'Of course.' She put down her pen and looked at him coolly, trying to hide the quick, absurd leap of her heart at the sight of him. At that moment she knew she was in love, and in spite of her racing pulses, her mind was warning her to stay calm, stay in control, use her head.

'I suppose you know there's a certain amount of talk about us,' he said. 'Does it bother you?'

She shrugged. 'It can't be helped. We have nothing to hide, have we?'

'No, we haven't. May I come round to your place tonight?'

It was the first time he had asked for permission, and she wondered if it indicated a shift in their relationship. Again she remembered his passion when he had kissed her on the island, and her own helpless, answering passion. Her body wanted to experience that again, but caution intervened. She wasn't sure what Russ would ask of her, expect of her. She wasn't sure of him, and she was very unsure of herself and her emotions. Her instinct was to trust him, but could she trust her instinct? Her feelings might be clouding her judgment.

'It might be better not,' she said, taking the cowardly way. 'We can't do anything about the gossip, but perhaps we needn't fuel it.'

He was silent for a moment. Then he said, 'Okay, if that's what you want. I don't see that what people say should matter, though. When *can* I see you again?'

'You're seeing me practically every day, here.'

He moved impatiently. 'You know what I mean. Would you come to my place?'

'No!'

He nodded, as though he had expected that. 'You're calling off the whole thing, is that it?' he asked her coldly. 'Because of a bit of talk.'

'I'm not doing anything of the kind,' she protested. 'I just think we should—cool things a little for a while.'

'Yes, well, you're pretty good at that, aren't you?'

'Don't be nasty!'

'I feel nasty. All right, I'm sorry. I'm going away tomorrow anyway.'

'Oh, yes—I'd forgotten.' He was attending a computer fair in Wellington, she remembered, to size up the opposition and help to publicise their own wares at the same time.

It would give her time to sort out her feelings, perhaps. Unable to disguise the relief in her voice, she said, 'You'll be away until the weekend, won't you? I'll see you next Monday, then.'

'Yes,' he said, his voice sounding clipped. 'I'll report back then.'

On the following Sunday Stella had promised to take her godchild, June's ten-year-old daughter, to the Easter Show held at Epsom each year. After a week of feeling depressed and confused, and no nearer to deciding how to handle her relationship with Russ, it was at least something to occupy her mind. The showgrounds were noisy and crowded, and young Tricia seemed blessed with boundless energy and a limitless capacity for enjoyment. Some of her zest rubbed off on Stella, as she shook off her depression and recklessly gave in to Tricia's pleas to go with her on the Big Dipper and the Ferris wheel, and to investigate the tents advertising mysterious magical acts, and of course the House of Horrors and the Palace of Mirrors.

They traversed the exhibition halls, admiring the up-to-date household equipment and sampling free drinks and foods, and Tricia collected a fistful of brochures with coloured pictures and diagrams of everything from milking machines to kitset doll's houses, and then they made their way to the sideshow alley, where an ecstatic Tricia won a particularly ugly green plaster frog for putting balls in the mouths of plaster clowns, and they spent a great many coins fruitlessly trying to make a pair of tongs in a glass case pick up a gold watch which Tricia coveted to desperation.

'Never mind,' Stella told her when at last they decided to give up, 'have a try at the hoopla. You might have better luck.'

There was a crowd around the stall, and while they waited for Tricia's turn, Stella looked about with a faint but despairing hope of finding some kind of seat. Her feet ached, and after several hours of hectic fun she was beginning to flag. Ruefully reflecting that she must be feeling her age, she found her gaze suddenly arrested by a familiar black head over at the stall where marksmen were trying to shoot down wooden ducks.

Her lips formed his name, 'Russ', as he pulled the trigger, and a girl who had been standing beside him suddenly squealed and flung her arms about his neck to plant a kiss squarely on his mouth. He held the rifle in one hand, but the other went round the girl's waist, and as their lips parted, he laughed down at her, before turning to the stallholder, who was passing him a large stuffed panda.

Grinning, he handed it to the girl, and she hugged him again and kissed his cheek, before grabbing at his hand and dragging him off to the next tent. Russ's head was turned to the girl as they passed within yards of Stella, but the girl's face, animated and happy, was clearly visible as she looked up at him. She couldn't have been older than eighteen, and she was dark and very, very pretty, with a clear complexion and big brown eyes, and a beautiful smile.

Stella stood perfectly still, getting colder and colder, until Tricia brought her back to a sense of the present, tugging at her arm and asking which target she should aim for.

Well, at least now she knew what to do, she told herself numbly later that night. Thank heaven she hadn't made too much of an idiot of herself, hadn't allowed Russ to know just how heavily she had fallen for him. And what foolishness! Maybe he was mildly attracted to her, and maybe he had an eye to the main chance, too. But at his age a beautiful young girl was, naturally, irresistible. She wondered how long he had known the girl, and whether she was the only one he had been seeing as well as herself. She was jealous, she realised painfully, and for a moment or two was tempted to confront him with her jealousy.

But that would be both undignified and unfair. He had made no commitment, no promises to her, and she didn't have any reason to question him. He had every right to take out as many girls as he wanted, and being young he probably enjoyed playing the field. He wasn't ready to settle for a serious relationship with just one woman.

But Stella didn't want to share him with anyone. She knew that there was no way she was going to be content to be just one of his girls. Thank heaven she had made no promises, no declarations, either, and at least she could get out of this mess with her pride intact.

He came in on Monday with a slightly wary light in his eyes, and gave her a report on the computer fair, his voice clipped and efficient, his face showing nothing.

When he had finished, she said, 'Thank you Russ. By the way, about that other matter——'

His head went up with a little jerk and his eyes narrowed. 'What other matter?'

'Well——' she looked down at her hands, tightly clasped on the desk before her, 'that—rather foolish gossip that of course had no foundation. In my position, you understand, I prefer to be rather— careful. It might be best if we didn't see each other again outside office hours.'

'I *won't* accept that,' he said quite quietly, but when she looked up, she saw that his eyes were dark and glittering.

Stiffly she returned, 'I'm afraid you'll have to accept it. It's my decision.'

'The hell with your decision!' he grated violently. He stood up, and Stella flinched in spite of herself, looking up at him.

Almost with contempt, he said, 'I'm not going to hurt you. You know I couldn't.'

She didn't know it. At the moment he looked capable of anything.

He leaned over the desk, his palms flat on the wood in front of her. '*Why?*' he demanded. 'And don't give me that—that *garbage* again about your *position!* If you care one iota about us, you won't be worried about what other people have to say. It's what *we* feel that counts.'

And what do you feel, Russ? she wondered with sudden pain. Was his anger the result of hurt pride, or chagrin that she hadn't been as easy a conquest as he hoped?

With determined calm she said, 'I don't see any point in discussing this further. I think you're making too much of it. I've enjoyed your company, and we had some fun together, but it isn't wise to continue to be too friendly outside working hours. You must see——'

'I *don't* see?' he argued. 'Are you telling me that when you were kissing me last week on Waiheke it was just a bit of fun?'

Faintly flushed, she shrugged. 'Basically.' Panicky, she wondered if she had given herself away then, responded too ardently, and if so, did Russ expect her to accord him an exclusivity that he wouldn't impose on himself? She wanted to ask him, but the blunt question would have exposed her too vulnerable emotions, told him too much about her feelings for him. She wouldn't sink her pride like that. Let him think that his company simply wasn't terribly important to her.

For a few moments there was a tense silence. Then, straightening away from the desk, Russ said flatly, 'I don't believe that.'

'I can't help what you believe,' she said, in strained tones. 'I admit I—encouraged you, and I'm sorry if I gave you the wrong idea. But a few kisses—surely we needn't get so serious about it?'

'*I* was serious, all right,' he said grimly, making her look up at him in fleeting hope, quickly hidden as she avoided the cold anger in his eyes. 'But obviously you're out of my league, Mrs Rawson. I'm not up to your sophisticated games. Did you indulge in them when you were married, too?'

Hope vanished in anger as Stella jumped up from her chair, white-faced and shaking. '*How dare you!*'

They glared at each other with naked hostility, and he said, 'I'm beginning to understand why Gavin Jepson got a bit rough. You'd been leading him on, too, hadn't you?'

'That's not true!'

'Isn't it?' he taunted bitterly. 'From where I stand, it looks all too true. What a fool I was! No wonder you kept reminding me of my callow youth. I must have seemed very small game to you.'

'Stop it, Russ!' she said, her voice sharp with pain. 'That's enough.'

He took a harsh, long-drawn breath. 'Yes, I guess there's no more to say. May I go now, *Mrs Rawson*?'

Stella didn't answer, and after a moment she heard him turn and leave, shutting the door very quietly behind him.

CHAPTER EIGHT

SOMETHING cold and hard seemed to have settled round her heart like a thick coating of ice. It was weeks since she had seen Russ without other people present, weeks since he had looked at her with anything other than a guarded hostility. She couldn't believe that she could feel this way about him, hurting every time she saw him, flinching away from his eyes because she couldn't bear to see him look at her like that, without any liking, any warmth.

She told herself that she would get over it, that it was only because she had to see him nearly every day that the pain was lasting so long. But it didn't help.

Owen said nothing, tactfully refraining from comment, but she knew he was relieved that she had cut off her private relationship with Russ. She noticed that some members of the staff were still casting covertly interested glances at her and Russ during staff meetings, but she carefully ignored them. There wasn't anything she could do. She tried to treat Russ with impersonal friendliness, and he was always chillingly polite. She hated it most when he adopted almost an air of deference, because underneath it she sensed a bitter mockery.

She was careful, too, not to be alone with Gavin. Fortunately he had other business interests which kept him out of her way a lot of the time, but he had asked her twice to go out with him, citing the loneliness of her widowhood, and hinting that she needed a fullblooded love affair to help her overcome it. Both times she had refused him, but the man had an insufferably thick skin. He had heard the rumours about Russ. When Stella told him tartly that contrary to his confident assertion she didn't feel any need for a man, he curled his lips scornfully and said, 'Come off it, Stella, you've spent a weekend with young Langford on Waiheke, and don't tell me that he didn't get you into bed.'

'As a matter of fact,' she said coldly, 'he didn't even try.'

He looked offensively disbelieving, and then surprised. 'Disappointing for you.'

'No, it was not!' she snapped. 'Russ issued a friendly invitation which I accepted for a quiet weekend away. I am not having an affair with him, and I'm not going to have one with you.'

'You could change your mind about that.'

Stella gritted her teeth, and sighed. 'I won't. I wish you'd realise I mean what I say.'

'No woman ever means what she says.'

It was typical of the way his mind worked, she thought. Maybe of the way all their minds worked. But just for a moment she wished Russ had shared some of his scepticism. If he had not believed she meant it when she refused to see him again except in a business capacity, she would have been tempted to weaken.

As though he had read her thoughts, Gavin said, 'Lover boy took you for real, did he?'

'What do you mean?' she asked unguardedly, her startled eyes meeting his.

'He thought you meant it when you told him not to touch, did he?' Gavin grinned. 'Or didn't you need to tell him? My guess is he respected your feelings, and never dared lay a finger on you. He's a boy, Stella. He doesn't know anything about women.'

Dispassionately, she eyed him, wondering how on earth he thought he knew so much about women himself. '*You* wouldn't respect a woman's feelings, would you Gavin?' she murmured, held by a sort of horrible fascination.

He laughed. 'My dear Stella, if you were honest with yourself, you'd admit that the last thing any real woman wants from a man is respect.'

Stella blinked incredulously. 'I guess I'm not a real woman, then,' she said dryly.

'You?' His eyes ran over her hungrily. 'You're all woman, Stella. And you need a grown man, not a boy. I know you've got a silly yen for Russ Langford, but——'

'I don't have any yen for Russ Langford,' she denied hotly. 'And I need no one, Gavin. Now please, if you have no more business matters to discuss, perhaps you'd leave. I'm very busy.'

Had she really made her feelings for Russ so obvious? she wondered after he had reluctantly left. Humiliated, she buried her face briefly in her hands. Surely Gavin was simply speaking out of jealousy and his injured male ego. He didn't really know anything about her emotions. In spite of his vaunted views on women and their needs he didn't really have any understanding of them—or, more especially, her.

One of the project development team, who had been on the original small staff when the company began, was throwing a twenty-first birthday party for his eldest son. Tom and his wife were pulling out all the stops, inviting a huge crowd of people to their rambling old home which they had spent the last ten years remodelling, doing all the work themselves on weekends and evenings. An engraved formal invitation arrived on Stella's desk, and although she had never felt less like attending a party, she answered the RSVP in the affirmative and spent the following Saturday morning in Parnell, shopping for a suitable present.

She went to the party alone, although the card had

specified 'and partner'. She didn't want a partner. She could have asked Owen, but felt that it wasn't fair to make use of the man when she had no intention of giving him anything in return. And although it crossed her mind that she could invite Gavin to partner her, she quickly dismissed the thought. She certainly didn't want to give him any encouragement. He hadn't, in fact, touched her since she had threatened his removal from the board, but he had said enough to make her certain he needed only the slightest hint of imagined encouragement to renew his unwelcome attentions. Those two were really the only unattached men she knew well. Most of her and Mark's friends had been couples, even those Mark had met through business. And she had very few invitations, because a lone female was a misfit at most social occasions. Some of the friends she and Mark had made she scarcely ever saw now.

Her dress was one she had had for a long time, but always felt good in. It was ankle-length, giving it a formal air, but made of very soft fine silk with a batik pattern of deep blue and black on pale blue. It left her shoulders bare and tied in a halter at the back of her neck.

The nights were cooler now, and she wore a black velvet jacket in the car, leaving it in the bedroom which had been designated a cloakroom for the evening, with a heap of other coats and wraps on one of the single beds.

The living room was crowded, and the double doors opening on to the dining room revealed that that room was equally so. There was a long, wide veranda running along the front and one side of the house, and after presenting her gift, congratulating the recipient and being given a drink by her host, she made her way through one of the French doors outside.

Coloured lights were strung along the roof edge,

and several couples were perched on the railing or leaning in corners, but it was a good deal less crowded than the inside of the house. It was slightly chillier, of course, but she preferred that to the overheated noise within.

She went to the railing and sipped at her drink, looking down at the well-kept garden. She and Mark had never had time for gardening, he had paid a man to do it all, but she knew that Tom and his wife tended every shrub and bulb themselves, and it showed. The garden was lovely. After Mark died she had of course been extra busy, but she had also taken over the garden, relegating the man to twice-a-month visits for lawnmowing and tidying, while she spent the hours between her snatched evening meal and darkness digging and planting and weeding. It had been therapeutic for her, helping her to fill the time when she would have been relaxing or going out with her husband.

'Hello, Mrs Rawson,' a clear young voice called behind her, and she turned, a smile ready, only to have it freeze on her face.

Michelle, the firm's receptionist, her bright young face framed in loose curls and her luscious figure outlined by a tight-fitting tube dress, that revealed most of her smooth nylon-clad thighs, had just come out of the house. And with her, his hand on her narrow, girlish little waist, was Russ. They were obviously together and Michelle, at least, was sparkling. Stella had never seen her looking so pretty.

'Hello, Michelle,' she managed to say, the smile aching as she kept it firmly pinned. Glancing up fleetingly, she added, 'Hello, Russ. Enjoying the party?'

'We've only just arrived,' he answered shortly. 'Michelle, shall we——'

But Michelle was saying eagerly, 'Have you seen the

presents? They're absolutely super! I saw the gorgeous shirt and tie you gave him. Real silk, isn't it, the shirt? I think it's lovely. How did you know what size to get?'

'I asked his mother.'

'Oh, of course. And did you see the painting?'

'I could hardly miss it,' said Stella. It was a large and rather garish nude which had dominated the table on which the presents were displayed, and she hadn't needed to go over and inspect them in order to notice it.

Michelle giggled. 'Tom says his wife didn't want to put it out, she's a bit shocked by it, but it was painted by a friend of Barry's, and he said he wouldn't hurt his friend's feelings for anything. He said if it didn't go on the table he wasn't having a party at all.'

'Really?' Stella murmured.

'Mm, he told us about it at lunch today, Tom, I mean. So of course I told Russ the first thing we had to do when we arrived was go and look at this famous painting! Didn't I?' She turned to Russ for confirmation, and he nodded, smiling down at her.

'Mind you,' Michelle added judiciously, 'I can see Mrs Kelly's *point*. I mean, some people might just be offended by it, I know *my* parents probably wouldn't like it, but then times have changed since they were my age, I keep telling them. Were *you* shocked, Mrs Rawson?'

'No, not at all,' Stella said truthfully. She realised that Michelle was nervous, she had been twisting her glass in her hands all the time she chatted on, and her eyes hardly ever met Stella's. She was probably wondering if Stella was upset by her appearing at the party with Russ. Or was she enjoying a sense of triumph? For a moment Stella felt quite shockingly malevolent. *Don't think you're one up on me, little girl. I could take him away from you like that, if I wanted . . .*

Horrified at herself, she pushed away the unworthy thought. Michelle was just out of her depth, dumped in a situation she didn't quite know how to get out of. Why didn't Russ take her away?

Well, she didn't need to stand here and endure it. Draining her glass, she said, 'I think I'll get another drink. See you two later.'

As she made to move, Russ held out his hand in a rather wooden gesture. 'I'll get it for you.'

'So the younger generation still have manners,' she remarked lightly, adding, 'No, it's all right, Russ, don't desert Michelle. Have a good time.'

She gave them a last brilliant smile, and hoped she had dispelled Michelle's misgivings. Hoped that the girl would believe that Russ was nothing to her but a younger colleague and employee.

But she wished passionately that she was not alone at the party. Of course she knew people, and as groups formed, split up and reformed, she was always included in one of them, but the fact of Russ turning up with a girl on his arm seemed to heighten her sense of being an unattached woman at a gathering where most people were in pairs. It was, somehow, vaguely humiliating.

There was dancing later in the evening, in a patio space which Tom and his sons had built at the back of the house. Tom, being the dutiful host, insisted on taking her out there and pushing her about the periphery of the flagged space, while the younger dancers gyrated and stamped and twisted in the centre.

'Don't really like this pop music,' he grumbled. 'I liked "Anniversary Waltz" and "The Loveliest Night of the Year"—real music. But the kids, of course——'

'They are playing this tape rather loudly,' she agreed. 'Won't the neighbours complain?'

He grinned. 'The neighbours are here. I will get

them to turn it down a bit, though. They'll be able to hear that six blocks away!'

When the song ended, he went over to do so, and Stella was wondering if she could melt away into the shrubbery and lose herself for a while, when a hand descended on her waist and Russ said, 'Dance with me, Stella.'

He propelled her on to the stone floor before she had recovered from her surprise enough to protest, and put both his hands on her waist, making her move with him in response to the music. 'Where's Michelle?' she asked him, and he jerked his head silently in answer. Looking in the direction he had indicated, she saw Michelle dancing with Barry, the birthday celebrant.

She had put her hands tentatively on his upper arms, not trying to pull out of his hold, but not encouraging him any closer, either. They had been dancing for a few minutes when he suddenly grasped her wrists and put them up behind his neck, dragging her into the circle of his arms.

She stiffened and said, 'Russ——'

'Don't say anything,' he breathed raggedly in her ear. 'Just dance.'

Someone dipped the already dim lights further, and the tune changed to a slower beat, and they were not the only ones dancing close to each other, held in each other's arms. *Yes*, she thought. *Just this once, for this little time, I want to be held by him.* She closed her eyes and blotted out all thought, only feeling his arms hard against her back, his thighs warm through the material of her skirt as they moved with hers.

The music went on without a break for a long time. When the tempo changed, he reluctantly released her, only to grasp her wrist and compel her into continuing the dance, differently now, dancing apart like the others on the floor, but with his adamantine gaze on her she suddenly felt reckless, uninhibited, a woman being watched with hard eyes by a man she wanted to make aware of her in every way.

Her head went up, and she began to sway her body sensuously, holding his eyes, watching the deep glow start in the depths of them, smiling at him, drooping her lids seductively, deliberately enticing him.

When he drew her to him again, still moving in time to the music, she knew she had succeeded. His fingers curved into her waist in a grip that was almost painful, and his breathing was uneven. Her primitive triumph was stabbed by a sense of shame. It was the first time in her life she had deliberately aroused a man without any intention of satisfying him. And she wasn't even sure why she had done it.

She pulled herself away with a suddenness that surprised him. 'Michelle will be looking for you,' she said in brittle tones. She eluded his hand and walked to the lighted area near the house, where Michelle was standing talking to Barry and one of his brothers, and drinking something dark and sparkly. 'I'm sorry, Michelle,' she apologised gaily as she approached them, 'I'm afraid I've been monopolising your partner. He's such a good dancer.'

Russ came up behind her, and without looking at him she said, 'That was fun, Russ. We must do it again some time.'

'You're good together,' Michelle put in brightly. 'I remember you at the staff party, doing that disco thing. It was great!'

'Thanks,' Stella smiled automatically.

Russ said, 'We were good together, but Stella got— tired of it.'

Stella threw a brilliant smile in his general direction. 'Young people have so much energy,' she said. 'Dance with Michelle. I'm sure she won't be so easily—tired.'

She didn't stay to watch them, but returned inside, and ended up helping Barry's mother and various aunts in the kitchen, heating up savouries and uncovering dishes for a lavish supper.

Soon after midnight, when she judged she could not be thought to be leaving early, she slipped into the front bedroom to retrieve her jacket. The room was in darkness, and she at first tried to find her jacket in the light coming in from the hall through the door that she had left ajar. However in the pile of coats she found it impossible, and groped on the wall for the light switch.

As it came on, making her blink, she heard a faint moan behind her and turned, going cold with horror. Michelle was lying supine on the other bed, with Russ sitting beside her, bent over the girl, his hand on her hair.

'I'm sorry!' she gasped. 'I didn't know——'

Averting her eyes, she providentially saw her jacket and dragged it out from the pile in front of her with clumsy haste. She reached up to switch out the light, and put her hand on the door to swing it wider. Her one thought was to get out of the room as fast as she could.

'Stella!' His voice was low, but it went through her like an electric shock.

Blindly she threw the door open and made to go out.

'Stella!' He grabbed at her arm, and she went rigid. Why did he have to stop her? Surely it would be better to pretend she hadn't seen them?

'Listen!' he said urgently. 'Michelle's had more to drink than she's used to—or someone's slipped her a Mickey Finn. The poor kid's been as sick as dog. I've just brought her back from the bathroom. I was going to phone for a taxi, but I don't like to leave her. Can you look after her for a few minutes for me?'

Stella stared at him, then went over to the bed. Michelle put a hand to her head and muttered something without opening her eyes. Even in the dim light Stella could see her greenish pallor, and the shine of sweat on her upper lip and forehead.

'Why a taxi?' she whispered, turning to Russ. 'You're not sending her home alone, are you?'

'Of course not,' he muttered impatiently. 'We came with the Wakefields in their car. My car's in dock.'

'I'll take her home,' said Stella. 'I was going, now, anyway. Do you think she can walk?'

'No, I'll have to carry her. We'll put her on the back seat, and I'll look after her.'

It was, she realised, the most sensible thing to do. When she got Michelle home, if the girl was still in her comatose condition, someone would be needed to carry her inside. And Russ, after all, had brought her to the party. It was up to him to see her home again.

He hoisted the girl easily in his arms, and they saw few people as he carried her through the wide hall to the door and then to Stella's car.

She drove carefully just within the speed limit, hearing only an occasional fretful moan from the back seat, and Russ's voice, low and soothing in reply, the words inaudible.

'Her parents will probably think I'm responsible for this,' he said once as she neared the address he had given her.

'Would you like me to come in with you and vouch for your character?'

'I don't need you holding my hand,' he said shortly.

When they stopped outside the modest suburban house, he said, 'Thanks, I'll manage now.'

As he lifted Michelle into his arms, Stella got out and said, 'I'm coming in. I want to be sure she's all right.'

They had to wake the girl's parents up to get in, and

after a succinct explanation from Russ, Stella helped Michelle's mother to put her to bed. Already her colour was better, and she opened her eyes long enough to complain, 'I feel awful!'

'She's not used to drink,' her mother said anxiously. 'We never have it in the house, and she usually only has a glass or two when she goes out. She's never been like this before.'

'It's possible some stupid fool thought it was funny to give her something stronger than she asked for,' Stella told her. 'They don't realise alcohol is a poison and can make people dangerously ill.'

'Do you think we should get a doctor?'

'I don't know. She does look much better. And Russ said she'd been sick, so she's probably got rid of a lot of it.'

'Well,' the woman said, 'we'll keep an eye on her. You've been very kind, Mrs Rawson. Thank you so much for bringing her home.'

'Not at all. I hope to see Michelle bright and breezy on Monday morning, but tell her if she's not feeling well to stay home and recover properly.'

'I'll tell her. That's very considerate of you.' She paused, her worried eyes returning to the girl in the bed. 'It wasn't Russ, was it? Slipping things into her drink, I mean?'

'I'm quite sure it wasn't,' Stella assured her.

'He seems a nice young man, but I only met him tonight when he called for Michelle. He works for you, too, doesn't he? So you'd know if he was that sort.'

'Yes, I'd know,' Stella replied, wondering how well she really knew him, but at the same time certain he had not had anything to do with this. He might be young, but he wasn't the sort of irresponsible lout who played idiotic tricks of that kind.

He asked if he could use the phone to call a taxi, and

Stella said swiftly, 'Don't be silly, Russ, I can drop you off.'

He looked about to argue, but in the end shrugged and muttered something that might have been thanks.

CHAPTER NINE

IN the car Russ said, 'I could still get a taxi if you'd like to drop me off at a phone box.'

'Don't you think you're carrying your aversion to my company to rather ridiculous lengths?' she asked him.

He looked at her sharply, and said, 'I just thought I'd save you more driving around in the middle of the night. If I had an aversion to your company, I needn't have asked you to dance earlier.'

Stella supposed that was true, but was aware that she had deliberately baited him after that. Deciding to sidestep a fruitless argument, she said, 'Tell me where you live.'

He shrugged and did so, and she started the car, the engine purring into life immediately and whisking them away from the kerb.

She drove in silence, concentrating all her attention on the road before her. It had rained since they left the party, a short, pelting shower that slicked the road, reflecting the street lights in greenish ribbons and making the red traffic signals splash colour on the tarmac. The tyres swished as they kicked up spurts of water, and the interior of the car seemed very warm and close in comparison with the fresh dampness outside.

Russ sat beside her without moving, not touching her, his safety-belt properly buckled, but she thought he had shifted a little sideways and was looking at her from time to time.

It made her nervous, and after a time, to break the silence, she asked, 'Did you enjoy the party?'

'Yes, thanks. Did you?'

A stupid, meaningless, platitudinous conversation, she thought.

She nodded, unwilling to prolong it, to play the polite game any longer. She wanted to ask him why he had brought Michelle instead of the the pert little brunette she had seen him with at the show, to ask him who that girl had been, what she meant to him— what Michelle meant to him. And she couldn't say any of that.

'You came alone,' he said. It was not a question, and she didn't answer that, either.

After a few minutes, he remarked, 'I thought you'd be with Gavin Jepson.'

'Why?' She couldn't resist that question, it came out without thinking.

He shrugged, and she reiterated, 'Why?'

'I know you said not, but I had the impression that what happened between you and me was—just an interruption. I thought you were his—girl.'

'I'm not a girl, and I'm not his,' she said flatly. She sensed that he was looking at her more keenly. In the darkness her face warmed. 'I haven't belonged to any man,' she said, 'since——'

'Your husband?'

'Yes, my husband.'

'He's dead.'

'I know it.'

'So, is there never going to be anyone else for you? You're not thirty yet.'

'I haven't found anyone else to measure up to Mark. When you've known the best, anything less isn't good enough.'

'He must have been quite a man.'

'He was,' Stella said with quiet pride.

Softly, Russ said, 'Tell me about him.'

She glanced at him for the first time, then. In the

dimness she couldn't see his expression, but his eyes seemed dark, very intent.

'He was special,' she said, almost unwillingly. 'The first time I saw him I knew that he was different from the other men I'd met. He was older than most of them, of course—already beginning to make his mark in the computer field, building up his business. He had—I don't know, a complete confidence in himself that had nothing to do with egotism. He just knew that whatever he wanted, he could have—because he was willing to put a lot of effort into getting it.'

'And he wanted you.'

'There was a heartbeat's pause. Then she said, 'Yes.'

'And you . . .?'

She gave a breathy ghost of a laugh. 'I wasn't too sure, at first. I wanted him all right, but I was rather scared—very young and not at all experienced. He tended to—overwhelm me. I was afraid he'd swamp me, take me over, make me into some sort of puppet, and I didn't want that. The first time he asked me to marry him I turned him down out of sheer fear. Then I cried all night because I thought that I'd lost him.'

'But he didn't give up.'

'I thought he had. He was so—well, so experienced, I suppose,' she admitted reluctantly. 'He stopped asking me out, and at work he looked through me as though I wasn't there. It went on for weeks—long enough for me to miss him quite horribly. A long time afterwards he told me he could hardly bear it himself. Then he kissed me unexpectedly, and I couldn't hide how I felt. Once he knew—that was the beginning of the end. And I needn't have worried. He never tried to smother me. He helped me to develop, grow up, find my own interests and my own level of competence. He was fantastic. He let me have my freedom in every way except——'

'Other men.'

'I never wanted any other men,' she said swiftly. 'Never. But yes—he wouldn't have stood for that. And I know,' she said, answering the unspoken question that now hung between them, 'that he never looked at another women after he married me.'

Russ didn't ask how she knew, or if she was sure. She felt his eyes flicker over her and then look away. Almost thinly he said, 'No wonder you're choosy about men. I take it Jepson doesn't measure up.'

'No one does,' Stella told him firmly.

'Okay.' He sounded slightly nettled. 'Present company not excepted. I already got that message, loud and clear.'

'I wasn't trying to get at you.'

'No? Well, warn me when you intend to try, won't you? I'd like to have time to take evasive action.'

Stella shook her head, unable to quell a smile. 'Sticks and stones,' she murmured. 'What I say can't hurt you.'

'Is that your considered opinion?' asked Russ, suddenly harsh.

Looking at him in surprise, she felt the smile die on her lips. 'I don't know what you mean.'

He laughed, a short, exasperated sound. 'Forget it. Turn left at the next corner.'

She negotiated the corner and drove along the street until he stopped her.

'Thanks,' he said. 'I could offer you a cup of coffee, but I don't suppose you'd accept it.'

She knew he was angry, and had only the faintest idea why. Irritated herself, she snapped, 'You don't know what I'd say if I had received a genuine invitation.'

The silence was fraught with tension. Then he said, 'Okay. Stella, would you like to come in for a cup of coffee?'

He expected her to refuse, of course. As she ought to, she knew. Instead she heard her own clipped voice saying, 'Thank you, I'd like that.'

His surprise showed in his utter stillness. Then he opened the buckle of his safety-belt and reached across to do the same for her. 'Right,' he said. 'Let's go.'

It was an upstairs flat, small, compact and modern. Stella sat on a tweed-covered two-seater sofa, and Russ disappeared through a door into the kitchen and she heard the subdued clatter of cups and spoons while she surveyed the décor. She liked the fitted oatmeal carpet and the heavily textured natural wool rug in rich brown and black and white that added an accent note to the floor, but wasn't sure about some violently abstract paintings that hung between the long windows on the outer wall. She got up to see them more closely, and was examining them when Russ returned with two steaming mugs in his hand. He put them down on the round polished wood table before the small sofa, and came over to join her.

'Like them?' he asked, indicating the paintings.

She looked a few moments longer at the long brush strokes of red and black that seemed to sweep across the canvas, as though each painting was only part of a much larger work which had some sort of life of its own outside the confines of the heavy wooden frames.

'I'm not sure,' she said cautiously. 'They're— exciting, but I don't know that I'd want to live with them. They're yours?'

'In the sense that I own them,' he said, and named the artist. 'Have you seen his work before?'

'No. Though I've heard of him, of course. He's making quite a name for himself, both here at home and overseas, isn't he?'

'That's right. I used to be at school with him. So I was interested when I saw these.'

'He must be young,' she commented, and intercepted a dry look from him. Hastily changing the subject, she looked about the room and into the glimpse of corridor she could see through one of the doors. 'Do you live alone?'

'Yes,' he said, his eyes mocking her. 'Are you bothered?'

'Of course not.'

'On the grounds that I'm too young to consititute a danger to you, I suppose.'

'I didn't mean——' she shrugged helplessly.

'No, you never do. Of course, it could be *my* virtue that's in danger. Do you have designs on my young innocence?'

His tone was aggressive, the anger not completely dissipated, but his eyes were inviting her to laugh with him, and she bit her lip to stop herself complying. 'I ought to slap your face,' she told him.

Something else warred with the laughter in his eyes. 'You do,' he said tauntingly, 'and see what it gets you!'

She could guess. This was dangerous, incredibly foolish. With an effort she dragged her eyes away from his.

'The coffee——' she said.

'Yes. It's getting cold.'

He sat beside her on the little sofa, and she wedged herself into the corner, sipping the hot, aromatic fluid and trying to pretend she wasn't acutely aware of his thigh only inches from hers.

He put down his cup abruptly, and Stella instinctively went rigid. Her fingers curled about her own cup, she looked at him warily as he settled back in his corner of the sofa, his arm on the raised back.

'You don't have to be scared of me,' he said. 'I'm only a boy, remember?'

'Stop it, Russ,' she sighed. 'I'm sorry if I hurt your pride——'

'Pride!' he muttered explosively. He got up and strode over to stand under the paintings on the wall. She had the oddest feeling that they reflected his emotions at that moment exactly, harsh and angry with a slashing violence about them. 'You have no idea what you do to me, have you?' he said strangely. 'Remember what happened on the beach at Waiheke?'

She flushed uncontrollably, holding the mug in her hands with whitened knuckles.

He said, his voice sounding raw, 'I don't usually—I usually have more self-control than that.'

'You don't have to explain——'

'I'm not explaining,' Russ said harshly. 'Not in the way you mean. I'm trying tell you—oh, what the hell!' He made a despairing, vehement gesture with his hand. 'You don't want to know, anyway.'

'Know what?' Her voice was strained, unnatural-sounding. She hadn't known she was going to say that, but the words hung there as though she could see them, waiting for him to react.

And then he looked straight at her, and said simply, 'That I love you.'

She thought that her heart did a double somersault. Carefully she put down the coffee cup, noting the satin sheen of the wooden table, the grain with its richer colours under the stain. 'You—you don't mean that,' she said weakly. 'You can't!'

'Why can't I?' he demanded. 'And spare me a speech about being too young to know my own mind,' he added sarcastically. 'I got over my puppy love stage before I turned twenty.'

She glanced at him fleetingly, and a vague anger stirred. He didn't look loving at all, he looked fed up and ready to hit someone. She stood up and said decisively, 'I think I'd better go. Thanks for the coffee.'

She thought he almost flinched. 'You can't just walk

away from it like that,' he said, sounding thoroughly exasperated.

Stella looked at him almost blankly. She was very confused. She couldn't believe what he had said to her. It wasn't possible that he meant it, surely? These three words were possibly the most debased in the language. They might mean anything from a lifetime commitment to another way of saying, 'Let's go to bed together.' *I love you* was meaningless without some qualifying addition, which he hadn't made. The temptation to reciprocate was strong for a few seconds, before caution intervened. She felt an imperative need to get away from him before her own feelings betrayed her.

Fiercely Russ said, 'I can go after what I want, too. Mark Rawson had no monopoly on determination. I want you, Stella—I want you terribly. I know you don't feel the same way—you've made that clear enough to me, God knows. But I'm telling you, I won't go away. Not again. I should have told you, when I said you couldn't whistle me back, that if you didn't send me away then, next time might be too late.'

'You don't know what you're saying——'

'I know. It's no use now to go back to your genteel, superior act, Stella. You froze me off with that once, but since Waiheke I know what's behind it—some of what's behind it, anyway. Can't you stop worrying about what people will say? You weren't totally indifferent when I kissed you, there's got to be something there for me—some sort of feeling, even if it isn't love.'

She was still standing by the coffee table, staring at him, feeling quite incapable of movement. Her voice almost a whisper, she said, 'You took Michelle to the party.'

He said, 'What?' and his face darkened in a puzzled frown, as though she had thrown in some totally irrelevant remark. 'Michelle?' Then he said, 'She's a kid! A nice, uncomplicated kid. She doesn't have a car, and mine is being repaired, and Maurice offered us both a lift, okay? So we arrived together, and——' he shrugged, '—we were sort of paired for the evening, I guess. And besides——' he stopped abruptly, looking oddly embarrassed.

'Besides what?' she asked.

He looked at her without speaking, and she suddenly realised that he had hoped to make her jealous. Again her heart seemed to be indulging in some peculiar revolutions. 'I see,' she said breathlessly.

'Pointless, wasn't it?' he said, his mouth twisting in self-derision.

'Not entirely,' Stella confessed.

Russ looked at her across the room. 'Not——?'

Stella shook her head, her eyes smiling ruefully, though her mouth was grave. She wanted to ask him about that other girl, but she had revealed perhaps too much already. A kind of selfconscious fear made her hesitate.

A spark of light had come into his eyes, and he came towards her without hurry, standing a foot or two away, not touching her. 'Stella?' he said interrogatively.

Afraid to meet his eyes, she was inspecting a button on his shirt.

She tried to remember that he was four—three—years younger than herself, that marriage to Mark had made her perhaps more mature than many women of her age. She deliberately recalled Mark's deep voice, the strands of grey that had already begun to appear at his temples before he turned forty, the tender, demanding skill of his lovemaking.

'What are you thinking?' Russ asked her.

She looked up and said, 'I was thinking about Mark.'

She wasn't prepared for the blaze of pure rage in his eyes, though in the split second before she felt his hard hands on her arms, dragging her towards him, she realised how provocative she had unconsciously been. Then Russ was kissing her, not gently, and instinctively she was fighting him, her hands beating against his shoulders, her head bent back under the pressure of his mouth as she tried to wrench away from his passionate assault. One of his hands left her shoulder to imprison her head so that she could not break free, the other slid to her waist and held her mercilessly while the punishing kiss went on and on until she was dizzy and breathless.

When he released her, she swayed, her hand automatically going to her bruised mouth, her eyes wide with shock and accusation.

He was pale, and his eyes glittered as he raised his hand and wiped the back of it across his own mouth that had gone hard and straight.

Stella realised she was trembling, and clenched her hands at her sides to try and stop it. She wanted to apologise for being tactless, cruel, unthinking. But the violence of his kiss had cancelled out the need for that.

Tightlipped, he said, 'You'd better go before I— forget myself even further, Mrs Rawson.' The title was like a knife wound, stabbing her so that she felt it as a physical pain.

She was quite unable to speak. She nodded, almost dazed, and looked away from him as he crossed the room and whipped open the outer door for her.

She passed him with her head held high, and without a backward glance went down the stairs and into the street and got into her car. Russ walked all the way down with her, and stood and watched as she drove away. Neither of them had said a word.

CHAPTER TEN

THE next morning Stella had the strangest conviction that the happenings of the previous night had been some sort of weird dream. But when she stepped out of her shower and saw herself in the bathroom mirror, her reflection showed a couple of bluish, smudged bruises on her shoulders where Russ had gripped her.

With a sort of shrinking fascination she touched them, her fingers lingering on the marks. He had said that he loved her, but he had kissed her with savage force, a violence that Mark had never used . . .

And yet she was aware that in spite of her instinctive fear and anger while she fought him, a fierce lick of desire had leapt into flame under his hands and his mouth. Even though he had hurt her, she had responded in some inexplicable way to the desperate passion behind the violence. And she knew she had no masochistic tendencies. The violent kiss that Gavin had forced on her had produced no feeling except angry revulsion.

It was Sunday, but she hadn't slept late. All the remainder of the night she had lain half awake, tormented by dreams and visions, and she stumbled out of bed at seven, hoping the shower would wake and refresh her, and grateful that she had the whole day in which to sort out the confusion of her thoughts. A day, too, in which she didn't need to see Russ.

She went to church, walking the mile or so there and back, obscurely hoping for guidance, for peace, for a quiet place to think.

Perhaps it helped a little, although her thoughts

were still muddled, but when she got back Russ was sitting on the doorstep—his head down, contemplating his linked hands between his parted knees, and looking oddly dejected.

He looked up as Stella came towards him, and got to his feet slowly, his eyes searching her face.

'I thought you were inside,' he said, 'pretending not to hear.'

'I've been to church.' She walked past him, put her key in the lock and opened the door. 'Are you coming in?'

He seemed to hesitate. It was the first time she remembered seeing him unsure of himself. Then he followed her in and pushed the door shut beind them.

She moved away from him immediately, going into the lounge. She didn't sit down, but stood stiffly by one of the blue chairs, her hand resting lightly on its back. She was wearing a linen dress with stitched lapels and cuffs, and high-heeled shoes with stockings, and in the hall she had put down a brown pigskin clutch bag that matched the shoes. Something in his eyes as they appraised her made her aware that she looked expensive and chic and very composed. His clothes were much less formal, faded jeans and a blue cotton shirt open at the neck, the sleeves rolled up above the elbows.

'Do you go to church regularly?' he asked her.

'Not exactly. But quite often.' More often since Mark had died. but she didn't tell him that.

He said, 'Did I hurt you last night?'

Stella shrugged. 'I have bruises.'

Russ flushed darkly, his voice harsh. 'I didn't mean to do that.'

Stella looked down at fingers curling now round the top of the chair. 'I know.'

'Do you want me to go?'

She looked up at him quickly, wondering if he

meant more than the simple words. She said, 'Have
you had breakfast?'

'No.' He looked back at her, his gaze steady,
expressionless—carefully expressionless, she thought.

'You might as well stay,' she said huskily. 'I was
just going to make myself some.'

It was a lie. She never ate breakfast on Sunday, only
a sort of belated brunch, usually toast and cheese or
some leftovers from the previous evening's meal. But
there were bacon and eggs in the refrigerator, and
while he set the kitchen table she cooked a hearty
breakfast for two. There was still a constraint between
them, and her voice was clipped as she told him where
to find the knives and forks, the plates, the marmalade.
She was glad that the sizzle of frying bacon covered
the inevitable gaps in conversation.

She poured orange juice and he made toast in the
gleaming pop up toaster, and as they sat opposite each
other eating the bacon and eggs, she thought that it
was like their Sunday morning on the island except
that they had been much more at ease with each other.

Well, whatever constraint there was, and it was still
there, it didn't seem to affect Russ's appetite, she
noticed somewhat ironically. But she, too, finished
what was on her plate and felt surprisingly better for
it.

She wanted to say, *Did you mean what you said last
night—that you love me?* But spectres rose to stop her.
Last night he had been drinking, although she
couldn't by any stretch of the imagination have called
him drunk. This morning he might not feel the same.
He had, after all, had a fairly stressful evening, looking
after Michelle and expecting to be blamed by her
parents for her condition. And Stella had helped him.
And then agreed to go into his flat for coffee. Perhaps
a combination of relief, drink and gratitude, along
with her ambiguous presence in his flat, had prompted

that declaration of love. Certainly he didn't seem about to repeat it.

Shamed, she wondered if he thought she had expected him to make some sort of pass—coming to his home at that hour, after practically issuing a challenge to him to invite her in, and then sparring with him as she had in that implicitly sexual verbal exhange. She couldn't remember now the exact words they had used, any detailed sequence of events, but quite possibly he had been going through the motions of playing the usual man-woman game. And—again the nagging thought that was never far from her mind intruded itself—he had never mentioned that other girl, the girl at the show. The girl he had been with, had kissed, at a time when Stella had imagined that all his attentions was concentrated on herself.

He pushed his plate away and met her eyes. His were dark and quite cool, with no hint of the angry desire they had held last night. 'Thank you,' he said. 'That was good.'

'Coffee?' she queried, getting up to take the plates to the sink.

'If you're having it.' He was very polite, the ideal guest. For a moment she wanted to scream. It was as if he was trying to make up for his savage behaviour of the previous night with an excess of civility this morning. There was an ice wall between them, and she felt quite powerless to breach it. Last night, if she had not made the fatal mistake of waiting too long, she might have said, 'I love you, too. I've loved you for weeks—perhaps months.' Now it was too late. She was too terribly unsure—unsure if he had meant it, unsure if she wasn't a monumental idiot and that if she confessed how she felt he would make of her an even bigger one. How could he, having his pick of younger and more vivacious women, have truly fallen in love with her—older, sobered by grief and responsibility, and bossy too, as he had pointed out on more than one occasion? Men didn't like bossy women, they labelled them aggressive, unfeminine and worse. Mark had encouraged her to be independent, but she had known better than to try too much assertiveness with her husband. He would never have allowed her to push him around.

And neither would Russ, she realised. He had always stood up to her in his own way, allowing her the prerogatives of a boss, but never letting her step over the proper boundaries, always showing her quite plainly and without fuss that in private he was his own man and not to be pushed too far—or at all.

In a moment of prescience she saw suddenly that he too sometimes overreacted, asserting the conventional male role very positively when he was with her, to save his own pride and preserve his masculine self-image. He wasn't looking for a surrogate mother, someone to run his life and tell him what to do and kiss his hurts better. In fact, unless it was the fact that by her very superiority of position she challenged him, she couldn't see any reason why he should be in love with her. Good looks, which she couldn't be unaware of possessing, weren't enough. He was too intelligent to have fallen for her face alone. Too intelligent to have fallen for her at all—unless her position in the firm was the attraction. Her money, her influence, her power—that might tempt an ambitious man.

She had been down that road before, but always the insidious suspicion returned. Gavin had suggested it crudely, Owen with more circumspection, but both were shrewd in business, both were men whose judgment Mark had trusted. If her own heart revolted against the suspicion, perhaps that was all the more reason to listen to them, because was she capable any longer of seeing the problem objectively, when Russ could make her heart race and her pulses throb with a mere touch of his fingers?

He helped her with the dishes and stood with a tea towel between his two hands, unconsciously twisting it. She took it from him gently with a little smile, an upward tilt of her eyebrows, and he smiled back with tight lips.

She hung the tea towel carefully on its narrow rail, smoothing the damp creases out. Behind her, Russ asked, 'What are you doing today?'

'I've got a good book from the library,' she said. 'I'm going to sit in the garden room off the patio and finish it. It's due back tomorrow.'

She turned to look out of the kitchen window. The garden room had been an addition of Mark's, a pleasant little sun-trap with lots of glass, the floor ceramic-tiled and surrounded by large plants in pots, furnished with two canvas chairs and a low table. They had spent a lot of time there at this time of the year, when the sun still had some warmth but the outside air tended to chill.

'I suppose,' Russ said, 'you wouldn't like to change your mind and come out with me?'

'Anywhere in particular?'

'Anywhere you like.'

She hesitated, then said calmly, 'No.' She heard the quick intake of his breath before she added, almost without volition, 'But you can join me, if you like. I'll even lend you a book.'

'I won't need a book,' he said, and she swung round to face him, guarded enquiry on her face. 'I had quite a night,' he reminded her. 'I'm likely to drop off to sleep. Will you mind?'

Stella shook her head. 'But if you snore,' she threatened lightly, 'I'll throw my book at you!'

He smiled. 'Library books are public property, aren't they? I won't snore.'

He didn't snore. He didn't sleep, either. Every time she glanced up from her book, he was blandly contemplating the garden outside, or inspecting, apparently with botanical fascination, one of the plants in the big tubs nearby. Yet she had a distinct and prickly conviction that most of the time he was looking at her. He had accepted some magazines she offered him to read, and glanced with interest along her bookshelves when she had told him to help himself to anything he fancied reading. But although he had stayed there perhaps half an hour, dipping into a few volumes, when he joined her in the garden room and took the other chair, he was carrying only the magazines. And after leafing in a desultory way through them, he had let them lie in his lap for the rest of the afternoon.

Immersed in her own book, Stella managed to ignore him for minutes at a time, but each time he stirred all her senses sprang to life, disturbing her concentration terribly. She gave no sign, never lifting her eyes from the printed pages before her, but the last part of the story failed to grip her as the first few chapters had when she was reading them on her own.

When she finally reached the last page and closed the book, he asked, 'Finished?'

Stella nodded, and he reached out a hand. 'May I?'

She handed over the book, and he read the cover blurb swiftly, then flipped it open and skimmed a few pages here and there. 'Looks interesting,' he commented.

'Yes, it was. Would you like a cup of tea?'

'I'll make it,' he said, getting up. 'That is, if you'll let me loose in your kitchen?'

Stella said, 'Be my guest. I'm feeling a bit lazy.' She stretched her arms and brought her hands down again to cradle her head, and almost gasped at the sudden blaze she saw in Russ's eyes.

It was hidden in a moment, and he turned away to go to the kitchen, but for several minutes Stella stayed like a stone statue, breathing shallowly, her heart thumping. Then she very carefully lowered her arms and laced her hands in her lap, frowning down at them.

Russ made the tea as she liked it, and when she commented, her voice light and firm, he shrugged and smiled and said casually, 'I remember—from Waiheke.' He had found some bread and tomatoes and ham, too, and made sandwiches. She realised with a pang of conscience that she hadn't offered him any lunch. She wasn't accustomed to having it on Sundays. She took a sandwich and put it on her saucer.

'I'm afraid I don't have a Scrabble board,' she said, sipping at the hot, refreshing liquid.

Russ smiled obliquely and said, 'What about that very handsome chess set that I saw in the lounge? Can you play?'

'Yes. Mark was keen. He brought that set back from Singapore. It's jade and gold.'

'Expensive.' His tone was dry, clipped.

'I suppose so. He never told me what it cost.'

There was a silence, then Stella put her teacup back in its saucer with a little clatter and said, 'Would you like a game?'

Looking at her over his cup, he said, 'Chess?'

'Of course,' she rejoined coolly. Her tone said, 'What else?'

He smiled, barely moving his lips, and gave a slight nod of his head. 'I should warn you,' he told her, 'I'm good.'

Challenged, she tipped her head up, her eyes meeting his with deliberation. 'Really?'

He laughed out loud. 'Shall I fetch the set?'

She nodded. 'Please.'

Russ stood up, looking down at her with an odd smile playing about his lips before he bent to take her cup and remove it with his to the kitchen.

He hadn't been boasting. He was good, and Stella had to keep all her wits about her to stay with the play. The game lasted for two hours, and when she finally lost to him, but honourably, she found that the strain had told. She felt exhausted.

'You weren't joking,' she said feelingly.

'You played well,' he reminded her.

'At top pitch,' she admitted. 'I have a feeling it wasn't too hard for you.'

He shrugged silently, and she said with mock bitterness, 'Go on, then, be modest.'

He grinned at her. 'Sore loser. Want a rematch?'

'Not on your life! Not today, at any rate.'

'Have I outstayed my welcome? I should be removing myself, I guess. Unless——' He began gathering up the exquisite chess pieces, his hands extraordinarily careful.

'Unless?' Stella prompted.

'I thought we might eat out tonight—let me repay your hospitality.'

'You don't need to do that.'

'I want to do that.'

The prospect was tempting. She knew that she didn't want to be bothered with making another meal, and she was feeling slightly hungry again in spite of the sandwich. She had only eaten one, leaving the rest for him.

All the reasons why she shouldn't rose up to confront her, her doubts, his failure to follow up on what he had said last night, what Owen—and Gavin— would say, the gossip at work reactivating itself if they were seen. But against all those was one starkly simply fact. *I want to do that*, he had said. What was incontrovertibly true was that she, too, wanted it.

They took his car, and he chose the restaurant without reference to her, taking charge of the evening. The place was licensed, and the management looked slightly askance at Russ's casual dress, but he stared down the elegant hostess on the reception counter, and she found a corner table for them without comment.

Stella asked for a chicken dish, and he ordered the same for himself with a sparkling wine to accompany it. They talked lightly, apparently easily, but there were undercurrents of tension, of uncertainty. The easy friendliness they had begun to re-establish throughout the day seemed to be disappearing in the public atmosphere of the restaurant. Stella caught a stranger's curious glance on them, summing them up, trying to figure out their connection with each other, she guessed, and even as she gave the woman her chilliest look in return, she wondered how conspicuous they were, she and Russ, if the gap in age was obvious to outsiders.

They talked and ate and drank but scarcely met each other's eyes. Stella felt as though she was a stranger looking at her own actions and at his. The two of them went through the motions of enjoying themselves, but there was nothing real about it, the whole thing seemed to be taking place on some stage.

On the way home, some of the sense of unreality left her. She wound down the window and let in a cool night breeze, and her senses shivered into wakefulness. She glanced sideways at Russ, and saw his profile against the intermittent glare of street lamps, his mouth set firmly, his chin jutting. When he changed gear his sleeve brushed her arm, and as he drew up before the house, and leaned across to undo her seatbelt, she caught the scent of his skin, his hair, his clothes.

She said, 'Thank you very much. I enjoyed that.'

He regarded her for a moment with slightly pursed lips, then said, 'It didn't work, did it?'

'I don't know what you mean. I've had a lovely evening.' Even to herself the words sounded stilted, insincere.

He shook his head. 'Don't pretend with me, Stella,' he said wearily, 'You've been doing it all night, and I can't stand it any more.'

'I haven't!' she protested. And then, tellingly, 'I didn't mean to. I'm just tired. After all, we were both up late last night.'

'Yes.' He paused, looking through the windscreen in front of him. 'Will you let me take you out again?'

'Yes.'

He turned to look at her, and she had the feeling he had been holding himself rigid. He relaxed now, and said simply, 'Thank you.'

She shook her head and reached for the door handle. He slid out and opened it for her from the outside and followed her up the path, standing aside while she found her key and inserted it in the lock.

She turned to him. 'Goodnight, Russ.'

His hand closed on her arm, and she didn't resist as he drew her closer. His kiss was infinitely gentle, and she knew he was deliberately trying to erase the memory of the night before. She stood acquiescent under it, savouring the piercing sweetness of his mouth moving with exquisite sensitivity over hers. Her hand came up and rested against his cheek, but she didn't kiss him back.

After he had gone her rational mind asked her what on earth she thought she was doing. She looked in the mirror as she removed her make-up and noted the first faint crease on the smoothness of her forehead, the tiny lines already appearing at the corners of her eyes, the firm maturity of a mouth that when she married Mark had been softly, sweetly girlish. Its contours were still feminine and perhaps alluring in a more sophisticated way, but surely a man in only his mid-twenties would find smooth skin and innocently tremulous lips more to his taste?

It was difficult to believe that Russ was serious in his pursuit. And, she reminded herself, her heart thudding hopefully, it had, after all, been a pursuit. She might have been unwise enough to fall in love with him, but she had not run after him. Still, she was almost morbidly afraid of allowing him to guess how much he had come to mean to her in such a short time. If, when she was with him, delight in his company made her forget all her fears and uncertainties, as soon as he left she was again prey to demons of doubt. He could not possibly want her on any sort of permanent basis, and she simply wasn't the type to accept a casual and impermanent liaison. All the future she could see was heartbreak, and yet some glimmer of hope and joy kept her in thrall to her emotions. She was not yet— ever? whispered some dim interior voice—prepared to give him up.

CHAPTER ELEVEN

STELLA decided to live each day as it came and spare no thought for tomorrow. She refused to examine the consequences of her decision, refused to consider the possibility of gossip, of Owen's disapproval, of Gavin's outraged jealousy. When Russ invited her to dine with him, go to a film or a show, or spend a lazy day on the beach, she accepted, enjoyed each occasion, and felt fully alive again after two years of half-life.

Of course there was speculation, although at work they were careful not to overstep the conventional bounds of the employer–employee relationship. Stella set the pace by adopting a brisk, no-nonsense air which seemed at times to amuse Russ, for there was often lurking laughter in his eyes, but he took his cue from her, allowing no hint of the personal to intrude within the office walls. Outside working hours they didn't attempt to hide the fact that they were often together, and inevitably they were seen and, being seen, reported on. And of course Owen was concerned, though he tactfully refrained from direct comment, for which Stella was grateful. And Gavin commented predictably, 'It won't last, darling. When you've finished playing with little boys, let me know if you're ready for a real man.'

She tried to ignore him. And that made him angry. He sniped at her continually with innuendoes about Russ's probable motives, and her own 'infatuation'. Stella had to admit that he had scrupulously kept his hands off her over the last weeks, and knew that his sneers were largely due to frustration. She felt a strong desire to get rid of him, but was restrained by the knowledge that he had kept to her condition not to touch her, and also that Mark had very much wanted him to be a board member. But she was growing irritably tired of his too frequent assertions that she was living in a fool's paradise and must one day come to her senses.

Once, when he found her alone in one of the demonstration rooms and started on the familiar theme, she snapped at him, goaded into retaliation. 'All right, so what if I do? In the meantime I'm enjoying myself. And I'll thank you to keep your opinion of my relationship with Russ Langford to yourself!'

She hadn't realised that Russ had come into the room while she was speaking, until a faintly discomfited look came into Gavin's eyes as he stared over her shoulder. She turned and saw Russ looking distinctly wooden, before Gavin laughed harshly and walked out.

Russ shut the door of the demonstration room behind him and queried, 'What was that all about?'

'Nothing, just Gavin being more than usually obnoxious.'

'I did hear my name mentioned.'

'So?' She looked at him coldly, unwilling to go into details.

A stubborn light that she recognised came into his eyes. 'So, don't I have a right to know what's been going on?'

'No,' she said shortly. 'It was a private conversation. Did you want to see me about something?'

'Yes, the Tarahanga Farms project. June told me you'd be here.' He paused. 'Don't come too much the boss-lady with me, Stella. It grates.'

Already ruffled by Gavin's barbs, and the fact that Russ had heard her discussing him, however unwillingly, with the other man, she reacted with unwonted temper. 'I *am* the boss around here,' she reminded him waspishly, 'and I'll thank you to remember it in working hours, Russ.'

He whitened, and for a moment she thought he was going to walk out. Then he said evenly, 'The Taharanga project—do you think we could go down and take Warwick through some of the programs we've come up with for him? We can install a system, teach him how to use the software we've designed for him, and let him play around with it for a while, see what his opinions and suggestions are.'

'Sounds like a good idea,' she said crisply. 'If we're ready to set it up, I suggest you get on to Warwick and ask him when it would suit him for you to go down there. You won't need me this time, will you?'

'Not really,' he said in clipped tones. 'But Warwick may want you to come. He likes having the boss-lady in on things.'

It was not a very subtle reminder of their previous disagreement, and Stella glared at him stonily as she said, 'Let me know what he says.'

She didn't see Russ again that day until she was leaving the building and making for her car in the small car park at the rear. He was lounging against the bonnet waiting for her, and stepped aside silently to let her open the door. He moved around to the passenger side and stood waiting again, and after a moment's hesitation she slid into the driver's seat and leaned over to unlock the other door.

He got in beside her, looked at his watch, and then unexpectedly hauled her into his arms and pressed a long, bruising, punitive kiss on her mouth.

In the last few weeks he had kissed her now and then, lightly, with gentleness. Never like this. She pushed against him with her hands, made a protesting sound deep in her throat, but she couldn't evade him, and he didn't even seem to notice her struggles.

When at last he let her go, she was breathing fast, angry and bewildered, and even a little frightened. Her voice low and trembling, she demanded, 'What on earth do you think you're doing?'

'It's after hours, isn't it?' he asked harshly. 'Time for the boss-lady to start *enjoying* herself.'

A car roared out of the park, and she looked after it, wondering if its occupants had seen the kiss. Hers and Russ's, several places distant, were now the only vehicles left. Her furious gaze returned to his face, and she saw that he was looking grimly angry and bitter.

'I didn't enjoy that! Get out of my car!' she said, her voice raw.

'No.'

She stared at him, aware that she had no way of forcing him out. 'What do you want?'

'There's an obvious answer to that. But I'll settle for a few honest answers from you.'

'To what? I don't owe you anything!'

Russ drew in his breath, and looked at her for a few minutes in silence. 'Well, perhaps that answers everything,' he said cryptically.

Her mind whirling, her emotions seesawing between anger and a fierce desire to cry, Stella watched in stunned silence as he got out and slammed the door. He walked across the intervening space between their two cars without looking back once, reversed out of the park, and left.

Stella was still sitting there half an hour later, staring ahead of her with a numbed heart and an iron determination not to shed a tear.

June handed her a note the next morning. If she had hoped for apologies, explainations, a softening, she would have been bitterly disappointed. It said merely,

Warwick says next week, any time it suits. He wants you to come.

She had to see him to arrange a day, but they talked like two strangers. She debated making an excuse, telling Warwick she wasn't able to make it. She resented feeling obliged to make the trip with Russ, knowing her presence wasn't really needed. But Warwick was co-operating with them fully on this project, giving them all the help that he could, and he was entitled to have the head of the firm give him the courtesy of showing a personal interest. Mark would have done it, she knew.

Putting it off as long as possible, she chose Friday, defending the choice on the grounds of other commitments that week. But she was not going to be persuaded into spending another weekend in the dreamily verdant atmosphere of the Waikato. This time it would be only a day trip, starting early in the morning, and they should arrive at Tarahanga well before lunch time.

When Russ said he would prefer to drive his car, the one provided by the firm, she didn't demur. She was tempted to argue, but bit her tongue, realising that it would be arguing simply for the sake of it, just to show him that she was still the boss.

For the first hour it rained, the hissing drizzle and the grey, windswept landscape matching her mood. Then the sun pushed through a widening slit in the cloud and the rain lifted away like a theatre curtain, retreating to the distant hills and leaving a sunlit countryside sparkling in its wake.

They spoke of nothing but business, her voice clipped and cool and his hard and unemotional. Glancing covertly at him, she thought he looked older now than when she had first seen him, and wondered if she, too, had aged. Soon she would be thirty, and with the prospect a nasty, cold shiver crawled slowly up her spine. Most of her friends—most of them had been Mark's friends—were over thirty. They didn't strike her as being markedly decrepit or enjoying life less than younger people, but there was a sort of superstitious dread in her musing, a conviction of time passing too fast, of youth slipping away.

The Waikato seemed particularly lush and green in the wake of a few showers. The cattle looked sleek and well fed, the sheep soap-powder-ad white and woolly. Tarahanga, when it came into sight, had an air of prosperous rural charm about its hills, clumps of trees and neat white buildings that epitomised the dairy heartland of the country, its rich soil, abundant rainfall and rolling contours.

By lunchtime the computer had been installed in Warwick's office and the software programs explained to him and a fascinated Marianne. The first run through had Warwick fumbling nervously with the keys, and Marianne jittering whenever a beep from the machine announced a wrong keystroke or an error in instructing the computer. But Russ patiently explained that the machine and the software were specially designed to be 'user friendly', forgiving of mistakes and guiding the beginner through a step-by-step progression to competence.

'The questions that come up on the screen have been programmed into plain English,' he told them. 'And most of the answers can be keyed in as a simple Yes or No by touching the Y and N keys. When more complicated answers are required, they're usually numbers which you take from your stock lists or the hard copy—that's the printed figures—which you already have, and simply type them in as asked for.'

As he demonstrated the first program, and encouraged them to try it for themselves, Stella retired to the window, leaning against the frame to watch. Russ was a good teacher, she realised, patient with their questions, even though to him the answers were elementary, and clear and concise in his explanations. Some of the technicians, and even salesmen, they had employed in the firm tended to blind people with science, frightening off potential customers with incomprehensible terms and unintelligible instructions. As he bent over, his hand on Marianne's shoulder while she sat before the computer and hesitantly constructed a costing graph, she felt a sudden access of great sadness. She had alienated him, sent him away angry with her, and she wasn't sure if he would come back this time. She had told herself there was no future in any relationship with him anyway, that he was probably only amusing himself between girl-friends, or enjoying the novelty of seeing an older woman. After the party, and before that hard, ruthless kiss of the other night, he had scarcely allowed any hint of passion to colour his attitude toward her. They had talked and laughed and even danced once or twice, and sometimes he had kissed her goodnight, but Stella had found the kisses somehow unsatisfying. He treated her rather as if she were an older sister whose company he enjoyed. Even the kisses weren't much different from those he might bestow on a sister.

Until that last one, which he had forced on her in anger. And since then he had stayed aloof from her.

Honestly, she said to herself, hadn't it been her own fault? She had snubbed him unmercifully that day, and that had been his revenge.

Marianne successfully completed the graph, and jumped up triumphantly to go and get their lunch ready. Leaving the two men with the computer, Stella accompanied her, and was soon slicing tomatoes and grating carrots while Marianne chatted happily and deftly put the finishing touches to a mouthwatering bacon and egg pie.

By the time they left the farm later in the afternoon, both the McLeods had an elementary working knowledge of how to use the computer, and were eager to experiment with the various programs. Stella had firmly declined a repeated invitation to stay longer, inventing a mythical social engagement for Saturday which Marianne fortunately accepted, but which Russ, she was fairly sure, didn't. In fact, when they drove away from the farm he commented, 'You aren't really tied up tomorrow, are you?'

'What makes you say that?'

He shrugged. 'It doesn't matter. I just had a feeling you were making excuses.'

Stella stared out the window at the road unwinding before them and said nothing.

They had just passed Cambridge, a pretty little town with a broad, tree-lined main street and a central lake contained in a deep crater surrounded by a charming park, when the car's engine suddenly coughed twice, sputtered, and died as Russ expertly coasted it to the grass verge.

Stella looked at him enquiringly, and he said, 'It isn't the petrol.'

'I know that.' They had filled up in the town just ten minutes ago. 'What I'd like to know is, what *is* it?'

He shrugged. 'Sounds like the same problem I had a while ago. It was supposed to have been fixed.'

He got out and looked under the bonnet. Stella opened her door and went round to join him. He checked some plugs and looked at wires, then said, 'Do you know anything about engines?'

Stella shook her head. 'Do you?'

'A bit. But it's not anything simple enough for me, as far as I can see. Go and start the engine, would you, please?'

She did while he fiddled, but the motor wouldn't catch, and eventually he said, 'I'd better thumb a lift back to Cambridge, I think, or at least find a phone, and rustle up a mechanic.'

'I'll come with you.'

Russ waved down the next car, and the man driving it took them to a garage on the outskirts of the town and left them there. It was getting on to five o'clock by the time the mechanic, after going out to tow the car in, gave them the bad news that it was a long job and couldn't be done until the following day.

'I'm sorry, Stella,' said Russ, shrugging.

'It's not your fault. We might get a bus back to Auckland.'

'Is that what you want to do?'

It wasn't. They had had a long day, and the prospect of finding out about buses and travelling home on one didn't appeal. 'We could stay here till morning, I suppose,' she said.

He cast her a quick, comprehending look and said, 'I suppose so. We don't have to go into the office tomorrow.'

Stella wondered if it was a way of reminding her that no one would ever know. 'Well,' she said, 'we'd better see about finding a hotel.'

The mechanic obliged them with names and the use of the phone, and even dropped them off on his way home to his wife and family. The receptionist looked at them with cynical eyes and said, 'A double?'

'Two singles,' Stella intervened swiftly, and signed the register with a firm hand before handing the pen to Russ. They collected their keys and then went out to buy toothbrushes and toiletries. Stella decided she could sleep in her slip, and she noticed that Russ didn't bother about buying pyjamas either.

They ate at the hotel and sat in the lounge later, watching television and flipping through magazines which neither of them had any interest in.

Stella waited through the late news bulletin and

stood up. She didn't feel sleepy, she felt restless and depressed, and when Russ asked, 'Going to bed?' she answered on the spur of the moment, 'No, for a walk.'

'I'll come, too,' he offered.

'You needn't.'

'It's late. You shouldn't go alone.'

'I'll be all right.'

'I'm coming.'

Their eyes clashed. *After working hours*, she thought. But they wouldn't be here if they hadn't been working, if the company car hadn't broken down. Still, he was coming, and she knew nothing she was going to say would stop him. It was best not to bother.

She hadn't come prepared for evening, thinking they would be back by the time the night cooled. Her thin jersey wasn't adequate for keeping out the cold, and as they walked in silence along the street, the shadows of the old spreading trees dipping about them, she shivered.

Russ was wearing a bomber jacket over his shirt. He stripped it off and put it about her shoulders, but she said, 'Please don't—you'll be cold.'

'I'm okay,' he said, and as she tried to slip it off her shoulders, his hands came down over hers and held them firmly. 'Leave it on.'

'Thank you,' she said, and when he took his hands away, pulled the jacket closer under her chin. It held the warmth of his body in its fabric, and a faint scent of him.

They reached the park about the lake and stepped on to the grass. Their footfalls were cushioned by its softness, and the only sound was the slight breeze ruffling the leaves of the trees. They stopped at the edge of the path leading down to the invisible lake. Stella thought she could hear a distant ripple, see a gleam of starlight on the water far below them.

'Could we go down?' she asked him, her voice hushed.

'It's dark, and the path is steep,' He paused. 'They say the lake is dying.'

Her head lifted sharply. 'Dying?'

'A combination of storm water run-off and pollution from the ducks. Apparently there are too many of them finding sanctuary here.'

'What a pity.' She felt incredibly sad. 'But surely——'

'It may not be too late. The Council is trying to save it.'

'I hope they do,' she said. She walked a little way down the path, sure now that she could just glimpse the water through the trees. 'I remember picnicking here once——'

'With Mark?'

She hesitated. It wasn't always wise to mention Mark in his hearing. 'Yes,' she said almost inaudibly. She turned to him suddenly, unaware that by moving she had walked into a gap where the trees' shadows receded, leaving her in a pool of pale light from the stars that hung thickly in the dark sky. 'Russ,' she said quickly, 'I'm sorry I was so horrible—I needn't have snapped at you. You had every right to be angry.'

Coming swiftly to her side, he touched her cheek with his fingers, then slipped an arm about her waist and kissed her temple. Stella sighed, and leaned her head on his shoulder, and together they looked down into the dappled darkness and listened to the peaceful, stealthy lapping of the water.

'It's not dead yet,' she murmured. 'I can hear it breathing.'

She felt his smile against the fine skin of her temple as he turned his mouth to her again.

The breeze freshened, and she looked up as the leaves in the nearby trees rustled against each other.

Leaning back on his arm, she could see the stars beyond the trees, a wisp of scudding cloud partially veiling them, then drifting away.

Russ gazed down at her face, framed by sleek pale gold hair, her lips parted and her eyes shining, reflecting the stars. She felt his arm tighten about her, and heard him say her name, then the stars were blotted out as he bent his head and took her lips blindingly, his mouth passionate, seeking, insistent.

She swayed against him, her lips opening under his silent, inexorable pleading. The jacket fell unheeded to the ground as he swung her closer, her body curved into the hard outline of his, her hand going to his shoulders, clinging, moving convulsively into his hair as he deepened the kiss, her response waking in him a rage of desire that she could not help being aware of.

Sudden voices and laughter interrupted them, and they realised they did not have the park to themselves. Russ released her quickly, and bent to pick up his jacket and drop it again about her shoulders. He took her arm and guided her under the shadowing trees out into the open, and they walked past another couple whose laughing conversation abruptly ceased as Russ nodded, 'Goodnight.'

Behind them the girl laughed, a smothered giggle, and Stella felt Russ's hand on her arm tighten momentarily.

She wanted to say something to him, but her tongue wouldn't move. When at last they reached the hotel and went upstairs to the bedrooms, she knew that a word, a look from her, would be sufficient to bring him to hers. One part of her desperately wanted to give him the word, the look, that would keep him by her side and in her bed. But when they reached her door, and he took his hand at last from her arm, she lowered her eyes and said, 'Goodnight, Russ.'

He stood there while she inserted her key and

opened the door. But as she made to go in, he caught at her hand and drew her back to him and into his arms. 'Goodnight,' he said, and kissed her again, a long, satisfying, somehow promising kiss. Then he let her go and went on down the passageway to his own room.

CHAPTER TWELVE

BUT that night marked another turning point in their relationship. Russ continued taking Stella out and coming to her home, but he came now unmistakably as a lover, not as a friend—or a brother. He touched her with a new possessiveness, and his kisses were the kisses of a man who had been given a right to kiss her, to hold her, to touch her with a lover's touch.

At work she treated him for the first time as an equal without selfconsciousness—much as she had always treated other senior staff, and realised that at last she was able to be natural with him. She had ceased to be defensive about being attracted to him, or about anyone—including himself—noticing the attraction. They lunched together frequently in the staff canteen, and though they never touched, she knew that no one seeing them could fail to be aware that they were close. She didn't care.

Gavin watched all this with disbelieving eyes. 'Does he think he can take Mark's place?' he asked her once. 'Are you going to let him?'

'No one can take Mark's place,' she said icily. 'Mark was Mark. Russ is Russ. And none of it is any of your business.'

'I'm a member of the board,' he reminded her. 'And what affects the company is my business.'

'I don't see how my—my friendship with Russ——'

'Friendship!' Gavin repeated derisively. 'Why don't you admit you're so hot for him that——'

Stella, who had been sitting behind her desk, shot to her feet. '*How dare you!* You dirty-minded creep!'

'Okay,' he said, 'maybe I could have put it in a more "refined" way, but the truth is, my girl, he's a clever boy on the make, and you were a sitting duck. He's wormed his way into your bed——'

'He has not!' Stella denied hotly, and sank her teeth into her lip as she realised she had told him far more than she had intended.

Gavin halted, his shrewd eyes arrested on her indignant face. 'Ah!' he said with hateful enlightenment. 'I see. Lover boy's even smarter than I thought. He's got you dangling, hasn't he, darling?' He laughed. 'Well, that's a reversal of sex roles if you like! He's too clever to give you everything before he's got a wedding ring on your finger. He wants the whole business, lock, stock and barrel, or at least an equal partnership.'

'That isn't——'

'Isn't it?' His eyes were hard, suspicious. 'He's young and—capable, isn't he? Why else would he hold out on you, Stella?'

Coldly she said, 'Doesn't it occur to you that it may be the other way round?'

A flicker of doubt entered his eyes. 'I know you can be a cold little bitch, Stella,' he conceded, making her mouth tighten with annoyance. 'If that's the way things are, I'd be careful if I were you. He might just get tired of the game. It isn't only you he wants—he's after all that goes with you. High stakes, Stella, and young men lack patience. I wouldn't like to see you hurt.'

Liar, she thought dispassionately. Gavin was doing his damnedest to hurt her right now, out of pique and a bruised masculine ego. 'I don't believe you,' she said coldly. 'And I don't want to listen to any more of this. On your way out,' she added pointedly, 'will you please tell June I'd like her to bring in the file on the Rogers Ltd. query?'

Stella tried to put the whole distasteful conversation out of her mind. But although she kept telling herself that Gavin's opinion wasn't worth a damn, that he was merely being nasty for the sake of it, his words had hit a nerve.

It was true that Russ had not 'got her into bed', nor shown any real determination to do so. He kissed her, long, drugging kisses that left her feverish with desire, and his hands lingered over her body almost reverently at times, as though she was a beautiful but fragile work of art that he wanted to admire and fondle without breaking. He liked to remove the pins from her hair and see it tumble silkily over her shoulders, the strands clinging to his sleeve as he put his arm about her and tipped her head back for him to kiss her mouth and trail his lips down to the intimate hollow between her taut breasts. And he would take her hands and slip them inside his opened shirt, asking her tacitly to return his caresses, his breathing quickening as she ran her fingers over his warm flesh.

His own hands would be cupping her breasts, or stroking her from shoulder to thigh, and sometimes he drew back from her a little to watch their passage, casting quick, half-smiling, enquiring glances at her flushed face, his eyes glazed with passion.

Sometimes she wondered if she ought to allow the intimacies they shared, wondered at what point she would find the willpower and determination to say no. And with a mixture of shame and excitement, doubted if she ever would.

But he never gave her that chance. Somehow it was always Russ who called a halt, shifting away from her, taking a few deep breaths and turning to her with a rueful smile in his eyes, the passion and desire erased from his face, except for a deep, almost hidden glow that remained in his eyes.

Stella found it vaguely humiliating, and infinitely

disturbing. She would go to bed in a daze after he left her, her body clamouring for the satisfaction he had not given her, and her dreams tormented by pictures of passionate encounters. There couldn't be any doubt that she was sexually attractive to him, she had ample evidence of that, but she was deeply afraid that she felt it more strongly than he did, that while she was headlong, irresistibly and wildly in love, Russ's emotions were in fact far less powerfully engaged.

She told herself it didn't matter, but it did. Stella had a healthy regard for her own self-respect. She shrank from the prospect of being the one who loved most, the one who did the kissing. With Mark, she had fallen in love and matched his passion in the end, but at first it had been he who was the pursuer, and she knew that he would not have wanted it otherwise. Mark had always enjoyed a challenge, and her frightened retreat after their first date had intrigued him. She had never let him know that sheer nervousness had dictated her panic flight, and in time he had conquered her reluctance and triumphantly borne her to the altar.

A smile lingered about her lips as she remembered. Dear Mark—the memories had ceased to hurt lately. She could recall shared moments of delight and promise without the wrenching grief of bereavement. Russ had done that for her, superimposed his own vital, youthful image over the fading picture of Mark's tough, urbane maturity.

When she was with him, no doubts clouded her sheer enjoyment of his personality, the pleasure she found, his absorption in her that was both stimulating and enormously reassuring, or the sensual excitement of those caresses that always stopped far short of fulfilment.

But Gavin's warning, in spite of her conscious determination to ignore it, nibbled away at her subconscious like a slow-acting poison. Once or twice when Russ took her in his arms it surfaced to the forefront of her mind, making her stiffen and causing him to draw back in surprise, asking, 'What's the matter?'

'Nothing,' she answered hurriedly, drawing his head down to hers. 'Nothing.' And within seconds the ugly thought had receded, thrust back by the pressure of his lips, the strength of his arms, drowned by the sound of the roaring pulses of passion in her ears.

She had almost forgotten about the girl at the Easter Show. It seemed so long ago. Winter was with them, now, the days grey and showery much of the time, the waters of the harbour a dull dark green, and Rangitoto often shrouded in mist, but on fine days emerging into the winter sunshine as a distant, sharply etched mound against a pale blue sky.

It was on one of these luminous wintry days, with sunshine that made people blink as they came out of their offices and shops, but with a shivery breeze sweeping up High Street, and blowing little bits of litter along the pavement, that Stella saw Russ talking to the girl outside a café not far from their office. Stella was returning from a business lunch which had not been notably successful, and when she saw Russ, the breeze ruffling his dark hair, his lips wearing a teasing smile, her mood momentarily lightened, her heart beginning to sing.

Then she saw that the smile was not for her, but for the small brunette smiling back at him, standing close, her hand on his sleeve, her eyes dancing with pleasure in his company.

She stopped dead, and a woman with a shopping basket swung round her on the narrow pavement, bumping her with the basket and snagging her tights, and, to add insult to injury, favouring her with a glare as she passed on.

Automatically Stella glanced down, grimacing as she noted the small, spreading hole in her tights just below one knee. Under her breath she let forth an unladylike expletive. When she looked up again, the girl was walking in her direction, and she froze, watching the slim young legs revealed by a frilled red and white spotted mini-skirt, then moving up to the equally frilly white long-sleeved blouse, and the smooth, doll-like features emphasised by a brilliantly painted mouth and carefully made up eyes. The make-up, Stella thought miserably, made her look even younger than she probably was, like a twelve-year-old in fancy dress—Little Bo-Peep to the life.

In her beige linen skirt that just brushed her knees, with a gold silk shirt and designer-made tweed jacket, very elegant and expensive Italian shoes and a matching bag, Stella felt suddenly middle-aged and dowdy. And the hole in her stocking didn't help.

The girl, perhaps feeling her painful scrutiny, looked at her curiously, the dark eyes sliding over her with indifference before she passed, and Stella forced herself to walk on.

Russ must have seen her. He was waiting for her as she came level with him, smiling. And she wanted to hit him, scream, make a scene right there in the middle of the street. Instead, she stretched her lips tautly in a determined, brittle, civilised imitation of a return smile, and asked, her voice raw with the effort to keep it steady, casual, uncaring, 'Who was that girl?'

'A friend. She's the sister of an old school friend of mine.'

He didn't volunteer any more information, and Stella bit her tongue in a fierce effort not fire questions at him. Sister of a school friend? Then how long had he known her? What was her name? What did she mean to him? Had they lunched together? By arrangement? Whose was the invitation? Did they lunch together often? Russ didn't always eat in the staff canteen. *What was the girl to him?*

She said, 'Did you enjoy your lunch?'

'Yes,' he said. 'How was yours? You were seeing Rogers, weren't you? Will he be buying, do you think?'

'No.' She wondered if his interest was a red herring, but it was not possible, now, to drag the conversation back to the subject of his—girl-friend? And if that painted child was his girl-friend, what did that make Stella?

Mountains out of molehills, she told herself sternly as she answered his questions, made herself go the through the motions of conducting a normal conversation. Ask him, you've got to ask him, another part of her mind clamoured. But certainly this was neither the time nor the place. They were entering the office building, and by tacit consent their personal lives were never allowed to intrude in office hours.

She didn't see Russ again that day. She had a dinner date in the evening with old friends who had known Mark since he and Sam Marsden, the host, had been at university together. They were one of the few couples who still invited her to their parties, and tonight they were celebrating their twentieth wedding anniversary. They had married young, and Mark had always said it was the obvious success of their union which had finally induced him to take the plunge into matrimony. Sam, ogling Stella shamelessly, would grin at his old friend in patent disbelief, sometimes adding a slightly ribald remark to underline his point, and Dorothy, his wife, her attractively freckled face crinkling into laughter, would aim a kick at her husband in playful reproof. It had become almost a ritual when they met for an evening, as they often had, and Stella had taken a strange delight in seeing her husband drop his sophistication and his business face and become almost as boyish as Sam had always, somehow, remained.

She had not mentioned Russ to them. Once or twice she had introduced him to people they had met when they were out in the evening, but had volunteered no information about him and had cut short the conversation as soon as she decently could. She didn't want to introduce him into her circle of friends, didn't want their precious time together dissipated in social chitchat. For, although she tried to thrust the uneasy thought into the background of her mind, she could not erase an unspoken conviction that their time together was limited by circumstance, that this golden haze in which she lived could not possibly be expected to last.

The evening was pleasant and unexciting, but filled with warmth. Several couples were there, and an unattached man who sat next to Stella at dinner, and had perhaps been invited to balance her as the unattached woman. But no one made a thing of it. She found him nice enough, and though he made it plain he would not be averse to pursuing the acquaintance, she was able to gracefully indicate her lack of interest without offending anyone.

When she was leaving, Dorothy helped her with her coat and said, 'I take it poor old Don didn't ring any bells for you.'

Stella laughed. 'Poor old Don, as you call him, seems to me to be doing just fine! I should say, from his conversation, he's a bachelor by choice. He travels, plays golf, has numerous business interests, I gather, but doesn't work too hard. He appears to be having a ball. You weren't matchmaking, were you, Dorothy?'

'No, of course not. But I thought you two might just hit it off. Don isn't a bachelor, actually. He was married for six months when he was only twenty-four. She died.'

'Oh, I'm sorry. He seems to have weathered it very well.'

'Yes. Though it took him a long time, and sometimes I wonder——' Dorothy paused, then said, her look suddenly keen, 'And how goes it with you, Stella? Are you all right?'

Stella touched her friend's arm. 'I'm fine,' she said gently. Then, her mind bringing her a sudden clear picture of Russ, she repeated, with a lilt in her voice, 'I'm fine—really.'

Dorothy's eyes widened, her smile knowing. 'I—see,' she said. 'Are we going to meet him?'

'I didn't say——'

Dorothy laughed. 'You didn't need to. There's only one thing that can bring that particular look to a woman's face. You're in love, and I'm glad for you. And Stella——' her face suddenly earnest, she touched Stella in her turn, '—I'm quite sure that Mark would be happy for you, too.'

'Thank you, Dorothy. You're a dear.' Stella hesitated, looking down at her hands, the fingers of her right hand toying with the diamond solitaire ring Mark had given her when she agreed to marry him.

Dorothy said, 'You do believe that, don't you? I know Mark would have been terribly upset if you'd looked at anyone else while you were married to him, but I'm sure that he wouldn't expect you to spend the rest of your life alone.'

'It's not that.' Stella raised her eyes and said, 'It's my birthday tomorrow.'

'That's right, I'd forgotten.'

'I'll be thirty,' Stella said starkly.

Dorothy's eyes crinkled in amusement. 'So——? Believe me, darling, it's not the end of the world. I know it seems like the beginning of the end, but there are actually distinct advantages to getting older. You get more confident; your judgment improves, or at least people begin to respect it; you're actually better at a lot of things——'

'He's only twenty-six.'

Dorothy's smile faded in astonishment. 'Oh.' Then, rallying, she said, 'Well, that's nothing. If he were thirty and you twenty-six, no one would think anything of it. In fact, in today's world, I don't think you'd raise many eyebrows by choosing a slightly younger man. It may be unusual, but it certainly isn't immoral. If you love him, and he loves you——'

'That's the trouble, really,' Stella confessed. 'I'm not sure he does.'

'Well!' For once Dorothy seemed nonplussed. 'Well, I expect you'll find out sooner or later. Only—be careful, won't you?' Stella looked at her enquiringly, and Dorothy shifted uncomfortably. 'You're sort of going from one extreme to the other. Mark was so much older than you—I can remember when he told us about you, he said you were so young he felt guilty, but he couldn't help himself. Now you've found a younger man—it isn't a sort of belated puppy love, is it, Stella? Something you should have got over and done with before falling in love for real, only Mark didn't give you the chance?'

'Don't you believe it can be real?' Stella demanded, feeling strangely let down, realising that she had counted on Dorothy, at least, to give her wholehearted support.

The older woman's face softened. 'Of course I do. I haven't met the young man, have I? What's his name?'

'Russ. He works for the firm.'

'I suppose you have a lot in common, then,' Dorothy said slowly. Stella could see the anxiety in her eyes. Dorothy knew that if he worked for the firm, it must be in some capacity junior to her own position.

Like Owen and Gavin, she wondering if he had an eye to the main chance.

Stella sighed. 'I suppose it's hard to understand,' she said, 'especially after Mark—but——'

'It's all right, you don't have to try and explain to me. Whatever you do, Sam and I will always be your friends. Only, for your sake, do be very sure before you commit yourself to anything, Stella. We'd hate to see you get hurt.'

Stella nodded, grateful for the frank advice given without prejudice. Dorothy, at least, had no axe to grind, no ego to protect.

On her desk next morning she found an enormous sheaf of flowers. 'Happy birthday,' June carolled, as Stella stopped in the doorway, surveying the splash of gold and red in its cellophane wrapping. 'Those came for you first thing. Gorgeous, aren't they?'

They were, and she stepped into the office to lift and admire the sheer beauty of the gladioli and carnations before finding the card tucked into the ribbon that held them. She wasn't conscious of her happy expectation until she read the message and her heart inexplicably plummeted. They were from Owen.

She took them out to June, a smile pinned carefully on her mouth, and said, 'Can you find a vase for them? I'll put them on my desk.'

She left the card where June could see it, and later Owen himself came in on some pretext and she was able to thank him.

'How did you remember?' she asked him, knowing that he was hopeless at recalling things like that.

He smiled sheepishly. 'I asked June to remind me. She's a good secretary.'

'She's mine, not yours,' Stella retorted without

malice. 'I might have known—still, it was a nice thought. Thank you.'

He looked down at his feet, and said, 'S'pose you've got a date for tonight?'

'No, actually,' she said absently, wondering where Russ was. He wouldn't know, of course, about her birthday. She had never mentioned the date to him, had in the last few months consciously striven, when she was with him, to forget the depressing subject of their respective ages.

'I booked a table, just in case,' Owen said diffidently, and looked up, his eyes gleaming with hope. 'If you'd like to have dinner with me——'

Mentally Stella kicked herself. She ought to have pretended to be busy; now if she turned him down he would be hurt, knowing she would prefer an evening alone to one with him. And that wasn't so. She liked Owen—only suppose Russ wanted to see her tonight?

Joltingly, she realised what she had come to— waiting about in case he wanted to be with her, turning down other invitations on the chance that he might ask her out instead——

Lovelorn, she thought. That was the only word for it—a word that conjured up pictures of pale drooping maidens wasting away with unrequited emotion. Revolted, she said briskly, 'I'd love to have dinner with you, Owen. I can't think of anything worse than spending my thirtieth birthday evening alone.'

CHAPTER THIRTEEN

HAUNTED by the image of the lovelorn maiden all morning, Stella had worked herself into a fine state of simmering resentment by the time Russ came into her office hours later. June had long since reached the stage of just waving him in if Stella had no one with her, and he entered unannounced while she was on the telephone to a supplier.

She indicated a chair, but he came over to the desk instead, sniffed at the flowers and tipped his head interestedly to read the card lying on the polished wood in front of the vase.

She put down the receiver and he said, 'You didn't tell me it was your birthday.'

'Should I have?'

He looked surprised at her cool tone, but said only, 'I'd have sent you roses.'

Red ones? she wondered. He wasn't saying, and in her present mood she was prepared to believe that he was deliberately baiting her, keeping her in a state of suspense.

'Can I see you tonight?' he asked her.

With what she realised was mean satisfaction, she said coolly, 'I've already accepted a dinner date, thanks. With Owen.'

He looked at her sharply. 'I see. Some other time, then.'

Stella inclined her head. 'Did you want me for something?'

Russ slanted her a sardonic look, but she studiously ignored it, keeping her business face firmly in place. He seemed to hesitate, shifting his feet slightly on the thick carpet, his hands thrust into his pockets. 'I thought I'd tell you,' he said deliberately at last, 'that I won't be staying on here once the Tarahanga project is completed.'

Shocked out of her calm, she asked, 'What do you mean?'

'I'll be moving on,' he said, stubbornly. 'As soon as I've completed the Tarahanga installation and overseen the software development for it. I'll be giving a month's notice, of course, but I thought it only fair to give you warning.'

Why? her mind was screaming. Was he telling her it was over between them? What did he mean by 'moving on'? What was he planning to do?

At least she could find that out. Her voice crackling, she asked, 'Have you had a better offer?'

'Not yet.'

What did that mean? Someone had been putting out feelers? He thought he could do better elsewhere? He wasn't happy here? *Or had he found himself getting in too deep in his relationship with the boss, and decided to cut his losses?*

'Do you——' She stopped to clear her dry throat. 'Do you have any plans?'

'Not immediate ones. It's too soon, anyway. There's about two months' work on the Tarahanga thing still. I have some possibilities in mind, though. I may——' He paused, and his eyes searched hers as though looking for a reaction. '——I've been invited back to the States.'

Something pounded against her temples. Her eyes locked with his, and she willed herself not to betray her hurt and shock. She nodded, unable to speak. Her mouth was tight and her throat ached.

'I wanted to see you tonight, Stella,' he said, his voice dropping to the low intimate tone he used in their more private conversations.

What had he been intending to say? Goodbye, and thanks for everything? She shook her head.

'You couldn't put Owen off?' he asked her.

'No.' At least her voice sounded firm again, thank goodness.

'Tomorrow, then?'

She was tempted to scream *No* at him. How could he do this to her so calmly, as if he was only giving notice on a job? But, damn him, she thought, he owed her an explanation, didn't he? 'All right, tomorrow,' she said tonelessly.

'I'll come to your place. Do you want to eat out?'

She didn't, but she didn't think she could bear the thought of cooking a dinner for two, either. She nodded, and knew he was disappointed. Let him be, she thought viciously. Disappointment is good for the soul.

She was distracted that evening, and felt sorry for Owen, trying desperately to infuse a note of gaiety into their outing. Smitten by conscience, she shook herself mentally and made an effort to live up to his expectations. She drank too much and instead of cheering her it made her slightly maudlin and inclined to tears. Owen steered her up the path to her door with tender solicitude before midnight, and said comfortingly, after he had opened the door with her key and switched on the hall light, 'You mustn't worry about being out of your twenties, Stella. It comes to us all, you know, and there are compensations.'

'I know,' she said. 'Everyone tells me so. It reminds me of swimmers who call to the ones on the sidelines, "Come on in, the water's fine." And when you get in, the water's absolutely freezing!'

Owen laughed. 'Yes, I see what you mean. But if it's any help, the water tends to get calmer on the other side of thirty.'

She wasn't sure if it was any help. But he was a

sweet man, and she loved him in a mild, fond sort of way, and his tie, as always, was crooked. She fixed it for him, very carefully, taking her time, and he stood patiently on her doorstep while she adjusted it to her satisfaction and finished with a little pat of her hand. When she made to move away and his arms came round her, she stayed obediently still. He wanted to kiss her, and she couldn't think of a single reason why he shouldn't. He had done his best to make her birthday enjoyable, and he deserved something in return. Besides, his arms about her were rather comforting, and his mouth on hers was warm and gentle and really quite nice.

He lifted his mouth and held her away from him, smiling down at her. Then he pulled her close, gave her a quick, affectionate hug, and pushed her inside.

At least the dinner and the wine had made her sleepy. She tumbled into bed a few minutes later and straight into a welcome oblivion.

When she walked past the reception desk in the morning, Russ was leaning on it talking to Michelle. The girl was sparkling at him in the way most girls did when he spoke to them, the way Stella had seen her doing at the party.

Michelle looked past him and said, 'Good morning, Mrs Rawson.'

'Good morning, Michelle,' she rejoined frostily, and swept past them as Russ straightened in time to watch her retreating back. What had they been talking about? she wondered. Had he seen Michelle socially since the party when she had been so violently ill? Or did he feel, now that he had given notice to Stella that he was leaving, that he was free from some sort of obligation? Lunching with the little brunette, and now chatting up Michelle in office hours—perhaps he had finally begun to feel stifled by Stella's feelings for him, and decided to cut loose. Her cheeks burned as the insidious thoughts made her inwardly writhe with embarrassment. Her imagination, she realised, was running riot, and she tried in vain to curb it, stay calm, wait until she could see him, hear him out, find out what was in his mind.

She had appointments all morning with clients, and at lunchtime she asked June to bring her something from the canteen. She was very busy, and she didn't know if she could meet Russ with equanimity if the eyes of all the staff were going to be on them.

She left early so that she wouldn't run into him on the way out, despising herself for cowardice but shrinking from the prospect of seeing him before he came for her tonight. She didn't think she could have maintained the pretence of a purely business façade today.

She dressed carefully for the evening, aware that her understated raw silk dress, gold pendant earrings and high-heeled woven leather shoes, her exquisitely discreet make-up and sleekly pinned hair, and the French perfume she dabbed on her pulse spots, were the equivalent of a Red Indian's warpaint, or the Maori warrior's fearsome *haka* performed with horrible grimaces and threatening gestures before the enemy—bravado, designed to boost her courage and fighting spirit. If Russ was going to administer a *coup de grâce*, she would receive it in style, without flinching, and make him very conscious of what he was giving up.

She was ready for him when he rang the bell, but she didn't immediately answer it. Standing perfectly still, she deliberately willed herself to calmness before she walked at a leisurely pace to the front door.

He didn't ring again, but waited for her to open the door to him, and when she did, he stepped forward and bent to kiss her.

Stella jerked her head aside so that his lips just brushed her cheek. When he stepped back, shutting the door with one hand, his eyes on her face, held a questioning frown.

'I've just finished putting on my make-up,' she said then cursed herself silently for making excuses.

'You look gorgeous,' he said, but the frown didn't lift.

She thanked him in brittle tones and asked, 'Do you want a drink before we go?'

'No, thanks.' She had turned her back to go into the bedroom and collect a jacket. Russ's voice sounded wary, as though he knew he'd better watch his step.

She came back, shrugging into the jacket, not waiting for him to help her, and said, 'I'm ready.'

'You're always ready on time,' he commented. 'It's an admirable trait in a woman.'

'In men, too,' she said, 'surely?'

He opened the door for her. 'Sure. It's just that some girls think it's smart to keep a man waiting.'

She wanted to ask him how many girls he had known, had dated. Instead she clamped her teeth together and waited for him to open the door of his car. The firm's car. She wondered what he would do without it, supposed that actually he had more than enough money to buy one. His salary was generous.

Stella scarcely noticed what they ate at dinner. It had been a mistake, she realised, to ask him to take her out. If he had wanted to broach the matter of his imminent departure over the soup or salad, she couldn't possibly have let him, with all the other diners about, the waiter interrupting with menus and the wine list, setting the dishes before them and whisking them away when they had finished. She didn't know if she could have mustered enough self-control to conduct the conversation with any degree of dignity.

She chatted inconsequentially, in exactly the same tones she had learned to use with business acquaintances whom she entertained, or allowed to entertain her, out of duty; people who basically bored her but whom she had to mix with because of her obligation to the firm.

Russ seemed to take his cues from her, responding to every trivial remark with the proper reply, and the evening took on a nightmare quality. Stella felt that they were actually two other people, not themselves at all but a couple of puppets that jerked to invisible strings in a meaningless comedy with no plot—no beginning, no middle and no end.

But the meal did at last end, and when he asked her if she wanted coffee she said, 'I'll make some at home.'

Relief flickered in his eyes, and she guessed he was as anxious to get away from the restaurant as she.

In the car, he said, 'I'm sorry it wasn't a success.'

'The meal was very nice,' she said politely.

Russ sighed and fell silent. She had a depressing feeling that they were replaying a conversation they had had once before.

'You are going to make coffee for two, I hope?' he asked her as the car drew up outside her home.

Tempted to say no and send him away, Stella gathered her courage and said, 'Yes, of course.' Better to get it over with, rather than have a sword dangling over her head any longer. Besides, there was a note in his voice that warned her he wouldn't be put off much longer.

Russ took the key from her and opened the door, and in the darkened hallway he put his arms about her and pulled her close, kissing her as though he was drowning.

For a second or two she tried to hold herself aloof, ignore the beating of her pulses, the passionate demand of his mouth. But some desperate need in him communicated itself to her, and she abandoned the attempt to resist, her body melting into his, her mouth parting, softening, answering his passion.

At last he moved his mouth away, sighed deeply, and muttered against her cheek, 'That's better.'

Her mind in turmoil, Stella stood within the circle of his arms, knowing she had given herself away utterly, but in her heart a cautious hope. Surely he wouldn't kiss her like that if he didn't mean it?

Russ stirred, his hand slipping under the jacket, caressing her back, and his lips pressed small kisses along her forehead, on her temple, then murmured against her mouth, 'Tell me you didn't kiss Owen Armstrong like that.'

'No,' she whispered, the touch of his mouth as her lips moved under it shooting a dagger of desire through her body. 'Never.'

He grunted in satisfaction, and opened his mouth over hers, sending her spinning in a vortex of sensual pleasure, so that it wasn't until several minutes later that she asked him drowsily, 'Whatever made you say that?'

'What?' His lips were on her ear now, nuzzling and nibbling, creating a delicious sensation that seemed to melt her bones.

'About kissing Owen.'

His arms tightened. 'I saw you last night. You kissed him goodnight, right here on the doorstep. I wanted to kill him.'

Jerked into awareness, Stella tipped back her head to stare at him. 'What were you doing—spying on us?'

His hold loosened a little. 'I meant to come in after he'd gone. I thought I couldn't wait until tonight. Then I saw you kiss him, and—I went away.'

'I didn't see your car,' she remarked.

'I walked over. I had all night.'

'And then went away without speaking to me?'

'I couldn't have talked to you then.'

He didn't elaborate, and slowly she eased apart from him. 'You were jealous,' she said.

He shrugged and turned, walking into the lounge and standing at one of the long windows in the darkness. She took off her jacket, leaving it on the hall table, and followed him, switching on the room light.

Russ turned then and faced her across the room, his eyes brooding.

Stella said, 'You're not the only one, you know.'

'What?'

'The girl you took to the Easter Show——'

'The Easter Show?'

He looked blank, and she said waspishly, 'Your old school pal's sister—the one you were lunching with last week. You were with her at the Show. I saw you kissing her.'

'*Kissing* her?'

He looked astounded, rousing her to anger. She heard her voice rising as she said, 'Surely you remember—or do you kiss so many girls that one or two might just slip your mind?'

Russ went on staring at her, then laughed incredulously. 'What do you think I am? Mandy's just a kid. She started at university this year, and I promised Fred I'd keep an eye on her. Sure I took her to the Show, but as for——' He halted, sudden comprehension dawning in his eyes. 'I won a teddy bear for her——'

'A panda,' Stella corrected him, automatically, then flushed as he cast a suddenly keen glance at her.

'Okay, a panda,' he conceded, his eyes not leaving her face. 'And she kissed me.'

'You seemed to be enjoying it.'

'I suppose I did. I like Mandy. She's a sweet, spontaneous sort of girl, but I can hardly even remember it. It wasn't important. Where were you?'

'Not far away. I took my goddaughter.'

'You should have spoken to me.'

'You seemed—occupied,' Stella said dryly.

She looked away from him, and he said, 'That was ages ago—you didn't say anything——' He paused, thinking back, frowning with concentration. 'That was when you said that you didn't think we should see each other again outside office hours. Was it because of *Mandy*?'

She didn't answer, her hand smoothing the leather back of one of the chairs, her head bent. Quietly, Russ said, 'Why didn't you ask me?'

She shook her head and said in a low voice, 'I didn't have the right, did I? I have no claims on you.'

He said, 'I'll give you the right any time you like.'

She looked up at him, and found him searching her face. He came over to her slowly and lifted her hand from the chair and pressed the palm to his mouth. 'You know I love you, Stella,' he said. 'Would you marry me?'

'Oh, Russ!' Her voice broke and she yearned towards him, to be caught up in his arms, his mouth finding hers, parting her lips to the sweet tide of passion that swept them. He lifted her off her feet and sat in the chair, holding her across his lap while he went on kissing her, one hand sweeping over her body in a comprehensive, sensuous survey, and coming to rest over her thumping heart.

She kissed him back with equal abandon, her hands sliding to his shoulders and then on to his chest, her fingers intruding into his shirt, unbuttoning as they went. He moved his mouth from hers and started greedily exploring her throat, and lower. She felt him shudder and laughed softly in his ear, her lips teasing the lobe, her tongue darting into the convolutions above. His hands on her tightened until she gasped, then suddenly he was pushing her away from him, sitting her down in the chair while he stood up, smoothing his tumbled hair with fingers that were not quite steady, his eyes glittering as they ran over her flushed face, the tendrils of pale hair sliding down her neck, the rumpled state of her dress where he had pushed it aside to give access for his kisses on her skin.

Huskily he said, 'Do I take it that means yes?'

She wished he hadn't stopped touching her. She felt chilled without his arms around her, and there was a coldness in her mind, a tiny frozen icy wedge of caution that reminded her of what Gavin had said. *He'll keep you dangling until he's put a wedding ring on your finger.* Even now he was breaking off their lovemaking, leaving her longing for more while he waited for an answer. And on the heels of one doubt, others crowded in. This morning he had said he was leaving, that he might go to the States. It almost seemed like an oblique threat, a way of warning her that if she didn't accept him on his condition he would cut his losses and go.

She didn't even formulate the thought, the words seemed to tumble out as the idea hit her in a blinding flash, the one way she could be sure of his love, because he would get nothing from it except herself. 'Not marriage, Russ,' she said.

She saw the tautening of his expression, and swiftly stood up, winding her arms about his waist, shamelessly pressing herself against him, her lips touching the beating pulse at the base of his throat, then wandering to his shoulder as her fingers pulled at the edge of his shirt. 'I love you,' she whispered. 'I want you.'

His hands came down and gripped her upper arms, pushing her away so that he could see her face. 'But you won't marry me?' he said harshly.

Stella shook her head. 'Just love me, Russ.'

Love me for myself, she was pleading silently. *Please*

*say it doesn't matter if I don't bring you my money,
Mark's business, a top position on the board, any of the
things you might expect if you married me.*

Already she was filled with dread, afraid she had
made an irretrievable mistake. Tentatively, she placed
her hands on his chest again, stroking the warm flesh
in a placatory gesture. Russ looked down and watched
what she was doing, but his hands hadn't moved from
her arms.

'You mean you're willing to sleep with me?' he
asked her.

'That's right,' she whispered through dry lips.

'I can have you without marrying you?'

Stella nodded, wishing he would stop putting it into
such crude words, making her offer sound cheap and
sordid.

'Let go my arms,' she said. 'Please hold me.'

His hands dropped, but he didn't hold her. She had
shifted closer to him, her head drooping against his
shoulder, her hands sliding round his back inside his
loosened shirt. But as she realised that he was standing
rock-still, his arms hanging at his sides, she made to
draw back, humiliated and afraid.

Even as she did so, Russ moved to bring her against
him again, his hand behind her compelling her into an
intimate embrace, and his mouth searching for hers,
pressing her head back until her throat arched
unbearably and her lips throbbed under the pressure
of his. It was a kiss without mercy, without
tenderness, without any semblance of respect for her,
and when he moved his hand over her his touch was
rough and insulting.

When he released her, she swayed where she stood,
one hand pressed against her swollen mouth, a sob
rising in her throat. His face was dark with colour, and
his voice was harsh. 'Thanks for the free sample,' he
said—and left her without another word.

CHAPTER FOURTEEN

UNABLE to face the thought of the office and the prospect of having to see Russ next day, Stella phoned in and told June she was unwell and was taking the day off. Cutting short the secretary's offers of help and expressions of concern, she said firmly, 'It's nothing serious, probably just something I ate. I'll be fine by tomorrow. No, don't come round, just rearrange my appointments and answer what letters you can.'

She found that moping at home didn't do her any good, either. Everywhere she looked she remembered Russ—sitting in that chair, making tea for her in her kitchen, carrying her case into the bedroom for her that very first time he had come here. It was like the weeks after Mark had died, the grief almost as sharp.

In self-defence she went shopping for a lot of things she really didn't need, and met Dorothy Marsden in a delicatessen, poring over shelves of pâté.

'Stella! What are you doing here on a weekday?'

Stella's smile was stiff. 'I'm playing truant from the office,' she admitted. 'I didn't feel like going in.'

'You do look a teeny bit peaky,' Dorothy said with concern, peering at her. 'You work too hard.'

'It isn't that,' Stella said under her breath, and picked up a small jar at random.

'Why don't you come home with me for lunch?' Dorothy suggested. 'We haven't had a cosy woman-to-woman chat for ages.'

Stella hesitated, then agreed. She didn't feel like a cosy chat, but she didn't want any more of her own company, either. That silent house with its silent ghosts would drive her crazy.

Over lunch she was distracted, and at last Dorothy leaned forward and, placing her hand over Stella's, said, 'Look, love, I don't want to be nosy, but I wish you'd tell me what's the matter. Couldn't I help?'

Stella shook her head. 'No one can help. I—I've made a mess of things, but it's all over now and—Oh, Dorothy, I don't think I can bear it!'

At last the whole story came out, culminating in Russ's proposal, and his reaction to her offer of love without marriage.

'So I guess,' she ended bitterly, 'Gavin was right all along. If he can't have my—my possessions, he doesn't want me.'

'Would you have gone through with it—your offer?' Dorothy asked.

Stella looked down at her hands. 'I'm not sure. I just wanted to hear him say it didn't matter—that he'd love me on any terms.'

'You were testing him.'

'I suppose so.'

'If he knew that, you can't really blame him for being upset.'

Stella looked up quickly, then back to her hands. 'I don't think he knew it. I think he was upset because I'd refused to marry him, and by myself I'm only the consolation prize.'

Dorothy pursed her lips. 'Is that what you *think*, or what you *feel*?'

'Oh, God!' Stella muttered, suddenly dropping her face into her hands. 'It's what my mind tells me—all I feel is that I love him and I don't know how I'm going to bear life without him. I desperately want to believe that he did mean it when he said he loved me. I thought—I *felt* that he meant it, last night.'

'Then why not trust your judgement? Perhaps he was just so disappointed that you wouldn't marry him that he didn't feel like settling for something less.'

'I don't know if my judgment is being skewed by my emotions,' Stella sighed.

'So you'll accept Gavin Jepson's judgment instead?' Watching Stella's face, Dorothy pressed on, 'I've never met the gentleman, but from one or two things you've mentioned, my guess is that his judgment is warped by jealousy anyway. Am I right?'

'Possibly,' Stella acknowledged.

'Look, Stella, I can't really advise you, but I would hate to see you pass up a second chance at happiness because of misplaced pride or mistaken suspicions. Something about this business doesn't seem to hang together. You know, love isn't always as—safe and certain as what you shared with Mark. Sometimes it's a leap in the dark, a gamble. You're the only one who can decide if you love Russ enough to take the leap or throw the dice. The ultimate question is not how much he loves you, but how much you love him.'

On her desk in the morning she found a sealed white envelope with a single sheet of paper inside, which was Russ's formal notice. He would guarantee to have the Tarahanga project on its feet within the month, and then he would 'terminate his employment'.

Stella read it three times and didn't take it in even then, although she was well aware of what it was.

She put it down and stared out of the window for a few minutes, seeing nothing. Then with a decisive movement she picked up the letter and walked out. 'I'll be away from my desk for a while,' she said to June as she passed. 'Just take any messages and stall everyone until I get back, will you?'

Russ was in his office alone, making some calculations on a large sheet of paper, his face grim and frowning. The grimness remained as he slowly put down his pen and got to his feet.

The step in the dark, she thought. The throw of the

dice. 'I think I may have made a mistake the other night,' she said. 'Would you—if I said I will marry you after all, would you withdraw this?'

He looked at the sheet of paper in her hand, then back to her face and said, 'No.'

Groping, she asked, 'Why not?'

She flinched from the look in his eyes, because it was almost one of hatred. Then he said bitterly, 'Oh, what the hell, you already know how I feel about you, anyway. I don't know why you want to twist the knife now, but—the night when I saw you, and you kissed me the way you did—the way you always do—I lost my head and made a fool of myself. I'd been telling myself for weeks that I'd be mad to even think of asking you to marry me—that I was mad to keep seeing you. But I couldn't keep away. And in the end I couldn't even stop myself from committing the ultimate idiocy.'

'Idiocy?' queried Stella.

'You know what I mean.'

'No. No, I don't know what you mean,' she said, her voice hard and high. 'You're not very flattering, Russ. I wish you'd explain.'

'Explain what?' he demanded harshly. 'That I knew all along it couldn't come to anything, that you were just indulging in a little fun?'

Her eyes widened in disbelief, her lips parting on a denial, but he didn't pause. 'I never meant to get in so deep, but I couldn't help myself. At first I wouldn't think about it, it was enough to be with you, but ultimately I knew we couldn't go on as we were. There had to be something more—or a complete break. I knew I wasn't going to leave you that night before I'd at least made you say just how you felt about me— well, I found out. I hadn't meant to blurt out a proposal like that, but it was certainly one way of discovering what I really mean to you.' His mouth twisted. 'Well, I did, didn't I? You turned me down—just as I expected.'

'What had you intended to say, Russ?'

He shrugged. 'That I was leaving the firm to give us a chance to meet on an equal footing. And that if you were just amusing yourself, you'd have to find someone else. Then, when I took you in my arms, you were so beautiful, so—loving. Though that's the wrong word, isn't it?'

'No, it isn't. I told you last night that I love you.'

His lip curled. 'Oh, yes. Enough to take me for your lover, not as your husband. I know how deeply you cared for your husband, Stella. I've never wanted to take that from you. But I had this wild fantasy that one day you'd love me as much, maybe more. I'm sorry, I suppose I should be grateful for the crumbs you're willing to throw my way. You can't help it if you don't feel for me what you did for him. But I can't stomach being second best. I didn't want a love affair, Stella. I wanted a lifetime.'

'I didn't understand,' Stella faltered.

'No,' he said. 'I don't suppose you did.'

'I—was trying to prove something,' she said, 'one way or another, and I thought last night that I had, but now—I'm not so sure.'

The silence between them seethed with unanswered questions. Russ looked down at the figures in front of him and asked, 'What did you think? That I was after your money—the directorship?'

'Something like that,' she admitted. 'It crossed my mind and I—I acted on impulse. I wanted to be certain—that it was only me you wanted.'

He looked up. 'I know what's being said, of course. In the beginning it didn't seem important. All I knew was that you delighted me, and I wanted to know you better. It didn't occur to me then that people would talk. Later, I knew the gossip was getting to you, and when you seemed to take notice I was angry at first. Then I tried to look at it from your point of view, and what I saw from there made me sick. I didn't know how to tell you that I was only interested in you—that I could only see you, not the business your husband had built up and left you with. I knew that anyway the question was pretty academic. You loved him so much, there was precious little chance for me, and you soon made it clear you could do without my company quite easily. But later you let me come close again, and I thought you'd decided to trust me.'

'I did mean to.'

'But last night—you still didn't trust me, did you?'

'I was wrong.'

He said, 'I heard you telling Gavin that you were only enjoying yourself with me. Well, that was okay, but I wanted more than that. In the end I knew that unless I could persuade you to marry me, I had to get out while I still could, start somewhere else—forget you if that was possible. And I was convinced you would never take me seriously enough to be my wife. You seemed determined to preserve some sort of distance, except—except when you were kissing me. But that night, when you started asking questions about Mandy—I began to hope. I thought, if she loves me she'll see that it's between us two. That no one else's opinion comes into it. And that's all those unimportant things amount to really—what other people will think.'

'I know,' she said. 'But it wasn't only that. It was— I didn't feel you could really love me. I'm too old for you, and too bossy, and——'

'You're perfect,' Russ said simply, and Stella caught her breath, staring at him, her eyes suddenly pricking with tears. 'I couldn't look at anyone else after you,' he told her. 'But if I stayed, it would tear me apart.'

'You said that if I changed my answer, you'd still leave.'

She thought that what she saw in his eyes might be the dawning of a cautious hope. He paused, and said almost absently, as though his brain was occupied elsewhere, 'Yes, I would. In spite of what I just said, I find I don't fancy being labelled as the man who married into the firm. I don't want any part of this company, whatever happens. If I stay in New Zealand I'll probably set myself up as a consultant. I have some capital and I can raise a loan for the rest.'

'If you stay in New Zealand? You mentioned the States.'

He shook his head. 'I said I'd had an offer.'

'Were you trying to frighten me?' she asked.

He blinked. 'I was just talking so that I wouldn't take you in my arms and tell you I couldn't bear not to see you every day. Trying to save face, I suppose, preserve some pride.'

'You frightened me,' she said.

There was a curious, breathtaking silence. 'Are you,' Russ said carefully, 'saying what I think you're saying?'

'I'm trying to say I love you,' she told him. 'More than I can bear. And that if you still want to marry me, there's nothing on this earth I want more.'

He moved then, with a swiftness that startled her, but as he came round the desk she flew into his arms, her own arms going round his waist.

'I thought,' he said, his voice muffled against her hair, 'when you asked me if it would make any difference if you changed your mind, that it was some sort of cruel tease.'

'Oh, Russ! How could you imagine I'd do a thing like that?'

As her head went back, her eyes reproaching him,

he said huskily, 'I'm not thinking very straight this morning.'

He kissed her and she responded with a hunger that matched his. He shifted to lean his thighs against the desk, bringing her in between them. His lips left her mouth to caress her throat. 'I love you,' he said. 'I thought you were only playing with me and I couldn't stand it, but I couldn't keep away. I still can't believe that you mean it.'

'I do,' she said fiercely, putting her hands on each side of his head, dragging it up so that she could look into his eyes. 'I do. You'd have known I wasn't playing, if you'd ever——'

He waited for her to go on, then said, 'What?'

Stella shook her head, dropping it against his shoulder while her hands slid to the back of his neck.

'If I'd made love to you completely?' he guessed.

She nodded. 'Why didn't you?'

'Would you have let me?'

She sighed. 'Probably,' she admitted, slightly shamefaced. 'But it was always you who called a halt. I never got the chance to say no.'

'If it had ever happened,' said Russ in a low voice, 'I knew I'd be enslaved for good. I was trying to hang on to what remnants I had left of sanity and self-preservation. Besides——'

'What?' She looked up at him, surprised to find him looking faintly embarrassed.

'In spite of my rational self, I always had this dream that one day you would love me and commit yourself to me and marry me. Were you a virgin when you married Mark?'

Stella nodded. 'Yes, actually.' Mark had been surprised and then delighted when she denied him before they were married. He had teased her about her romantic ideals, but she knew that he had loved knowing he was first with her.

'Well,' said Russ, rubbing his cheek against her hair, 'I've got this romantic notion, you see,' he added, almost echoing her thoughts, 'about commitment. I told you I'd got over my puppy love days. They were very innocent little affairs. And I hadn't found anyone I wanted to commit myself to until I met you.'

She stood very still while his meaning sank in, then raised her eyes to his and searched them. 'I—never guessed,' she said.

'Do you mind?'

Touched, she framed his face with her hands. 'Mind?' she said softly. 'How could I mind?' She knew she was incredibly fortunate. 'Oh, Russ!' she sighed, 'I'm sorry I'm not——'

'Don't be silly!' he told her firmly, and kissed her mouth with dark force. 'You're everything I want. Everything I'll ever want.'

His letter of resignation had fluttered to the floor. Stella felt her foot stirring the paper, and moved away from him to pick it up.

'You want me to accept this?' she asked him.

Russ nodded firmly. 'I'll make my own way,' he said. 'And don't get any notions about making me loans or anything else. We'll be married, but that's a personal thing, nothing to do with business.'

'You don't want me to give up running Rawson's?'

'No, of course not! Unless it's what you want?'

'We might have children. I'm not too old.'

'Of course you're not too old. I hope we do.'

'I think I'd want to stay home and look after them while they're small. That's what Mark and I——'

She stopped and looked at him almost nervously. But the mention of Mark apparently had no power to hurt him now. He smiled at her and said, 'Whatever you want. In that area you'll still be the boss.'

Stella carefully folded the paper in her hands and said formally, 'Very well, Mr Langford, I accept your resignation. The firm will be sorry to lose you, but I'm sure you will be very successful in your new— life.'

'Thank you, ma'am,' he said, bowing his head in mock deference. Then he took the paper from her, tossed it on to his desk, and pulled her into his arms.

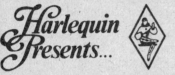

Your **FREE** gift **includes**

Anne Mather—Born out of Love
Violet Winspear—Time of the Temptress
Charlotte Lamb—Man's World
Sally Wentworth—Say Hello to Yesterday

FREE Gift Certificate
and subscription reservation

Mail this coupon today!

Harlequin Reader Service

In the U.S.A.
2504 West Southern Ave.
Tempe, AZ 85282

In Canada
P.O. Box 2800, Postal Station A
5170 Yonge Street,
Willowdale, Ont. M2N 5T5

Please send me my 4 Harlequin Presents books free. Also, reserve a subscription to the 8 new Harlequin Presents novels published each month. Each month I will receive 8 new Presents novels at the low price of $1.75 each [*Total— $14.00 a month*]. There are no shipping and handling or any other hidden charges. I am free to cancel at any time, but even if I do, these first 4 books are still mine to keep absolutely FREE without any obligation.   **108 BPP CAEE**

NAME _____ (PLEASE PRINT)

ADDRESS _____ APT. NO. ___

CITY _____

STATE/PROV _____ ZIP/POSTAL CODE _____ P-SUB-3X

Offer expires March 31, 1985